Praise for Barbara McCauley's SECRETS!

"Ms. McCauley does a splendid job of producing heroes to die for. This scrumptious series is a keeper to read again and again."
—*Rendezvous*

"Barbara McCauley makes our hearts sing with delight, with zesty interplay and searing passion all wrapped up in a marvelous love story."
—Melinda Helfer, *Romantic Times Magazine*

"Ms. McCauley's latest series is a hit. Fans, old and new, will be delighted with this one."
—*Rendezvous*

You loved *Blackhawk's Sweet Revenge*, *Secret Baby Santos* and *Killian's Passion*. Now Barbara McCauley brings her fans another scintillating book

Callan's Proposition

And look for the next installment as the SECRETS! series continues this August in Silhouette Intimate Moments.

Dear Reader,

This April of our 20th anniversary year, Silhouette will continue to shower you with powerful, passionate, provocative love stories!

Cait London offers an irresistible MAN OF THE MONTH, *Last Dance,* which also launches her brand-new miniseries FREEDOM VALLEY. Sparks fly when a strong woman tries to fight her feelings for the rugged man who's returned from her past. *Night Music* is another winner from BJ James's popular BLACK WATCH series. Read this touching story about two wounded souls who find redeeming love in each other's arms.

Anne Marie Winston returns to Desire with her emotionally provocative *Seduction, Cowboy Style,* about an alpha male cowboy who seeks revenge by seducing his enemy's sister. In *The Barons of Texas: Jill* by Fayrene Preston, THE BARONS OF TEXAS miniseries offers another feisty sister, and the sexy Texan who claims her.

Desire's theme promotion THE BABY BANK, in which interesting events occur on the way to the sperm bank, continues with Katherine Garbera's *Her Baby's Father.* And Barbara McCauley's scandalously sexy miniseries SECRETS! offers another tantalizing tale with *Callan's Proposition,* featuring a boss who masquerades as his secretary's fiancé.

Please join in the celebration of Silhouette's 20th anniversary by indulging in all six Desire titles—which will fulfill *your* every desire!

Enjoy!

Joan Marlow Golan

Joan Marlow Golan
Senior Editor, Silhouette Desire

Please address questions and book requests to:
Silhouette Reader Service
U.S.: 3010 Walden Ave., P.O. Box 1325, Buffalo, NY 14269
Canadian: P.O. Box 609, Fort Erie, Ont. L2A 5X3

Callan's Proposition
BARBARA McCAULEY

Published by Silhouette Books
America's Publisher of Contemporary Romance

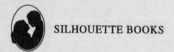 **SILHOUETTE BOOKS**

ISBN 0-373-76290-9

CALLAN'S PROPOSITION

Books by Barbara McCauley

Silhouette Desire

Woman Tamer #621
Man from Cougar Pass #698
Her Kind of Man #771
Whitehorn's Woman #803
A Man Like Cade #832
Nightfire #875
*Texas Heat #917
*Texas Temptation #948
*Texas Pride #971
Midnight Bride #1028
The Nanny and the Reluctant Rancher #1066
Courtship in Granite Ridge #1128
Seduction of the Reluctant Bride #1144
†Blackhawk's Sweet Revenge #1230
†Secret Baby Santos #1236
†Killian's Passion #1242
†Callan's Proposition #1290

*Hearts of Stone
†Secrets!

BARBARA McCAULEY

was born and raised in California and has spent a good portion of her life exploring the mountains, beaches and deserts so abundant there. The youngest of five children, she grew up in a small house, and her only chance for a moment alone was to sneak into the backyard with a book and quietly hide away.

With two children of her own now and a busy household, she still finds herself slipping away to enjoy a good novel. A daydreamer and incurable romantic, she says writing has fulfilled her most incredible dream of all— breathing life into the people in her mind and making them real. She has one loud and demanding Amazon parrot named Fred and a German shepherd named Max. When she can manage the time, she loves to sink her hands into freshly-turned soil and make things grow.

One

Hot shower. Cold Beer. Woman.

Callan Sinclair sighed just thinking about the top three items on his "to do" list. After four hours of wading through rain and mud at the construction site in Woodbury, thirty minutes changing a flat on his truck, then nearly four hours on the road, Callan knew that the shower should come first. His jeans and boots were covered with dried mud, and a fine layer of concrete dust made his hair look gray instead of black. And with a throat that felt like a feather duster, the beer would be right behind.

He could see himself now, sitting on a stool at his brother Reese's tavern, a tall, frothy ale in an ice-covered mug in his hand, a ball game on the overhead television and Bonnie Raitt blasting from the jukebox. He could almost hear her deep, throaty moan about love gone wrong.

He could probably leave the woman part of his "list" until the morning, Callan thought as he trudged up the stairs to his second-story office, but Abigail, his secretary, had seemed determined to reach him. She'd paged him three times this morning while he was still at the job site, but he'd forgotten to charge his cell phone the night before and the battery had gone dead.

Whatever the crisis was, Callan was certain that his secretary could take care of it. Behind her tight blond bun, oversize glasses and tailored suits was the most organized, efficient, competent secretary in the world. During the year she'd worked for him, she'd always been on time, was never moody or subject to emotional outbursts, was terrific with the clients and best of all, she never bothered him with annoying chatter about her personal life.

Cal didn't even think she *had* a personal life. He supposed that most people would consider her dull, but what did he care? To him, Abigail Thomas was perfect in every way that mattered.

Cal glanced at his watch as he reached for the office door. It was four o'clock, so he had time to handle whatever problem Abigail might be having, stop by his apartment for a shower, then get over to the tavern for a beer. Maybe he'd give Shelly Michaels a call, see if she wanted to join him. He hadn't had much time for female companionship lately, but he and Shelly saw each other from time to time. She was sexy and fun and didn't think about wedding rings if a guy asked her out more than once. At thirty-three, Cal knew he should be thinking about settling down, but he wasn't quite ready for the Big Squeeze yet. Maybe another year or two. Or three. Besides, he'd always thought that Gabe, being the oldest, should be the first to jump into those cold, deep waters. To go boldly where no man had gone before—or in this case, no Sinclair man.

So for now, the only steady woman in Callan's life was his secretary. Dependable, reliable, steadfast Abigail.

She'd worked for him almost a year now, well, technically for Sinclair Construction, but Gabe handled renovations and remodels and was rarely in the office, and Lucian was site foreman and used his trailer as his office. Which left Callan in charge of development and running the main office, which he knew very little about because that was Abigail's job. Since Sinclair Construction had opened its door five years ago, they had gone through countless secretaries, five in the past two years alone. And then Abigail had walked in, and he knew he'd found a gem. She was definitely a dream come true.

When he opened his office door, he blinked twice, then looked back at the sign on the door. Sinclair Construction. He had the right office.

But not the right woman.

A petite brunette with very large breasts, dressed in a very low-cut, very tight, pink top sat behind Abigail's desk. She was talking on the phone, and when she saw him, she raised one very long, very red fingernail as a signal for him to wait a minute.

What the hell?

The woman wasn't the only thing wrong here, Cal thought in disbelief. So was the office. Mail spilled over the top of the desk; manila folders were spread out on the waiting area armchairs; file cabinet drawers were wide open. A makeshift clothesline of white string stretched from the top of his inner office door to the top of his brother Gabe's office door. Paper-clipped to it was a set of architectural blueprints covered with brown stains. There was also a faint smell of something burning.

"Didn't I tell Tina that Joe Gastoni was bad news," the brunette was saying into the phone. "But does she listen to her best friend? Of course not, so now she's crying her eyes out, poor thing."

The brunette glanced up again from her call, and Cal frowned darkly at her. He started to move toward the desk, but stumbled over a package lying in the middle of the floor. The earthy swearword he muttered had the brunette sitting up straight.

"Gotta go, Sue. I'll call you later." She hung up the phone and smiled. "May I help you?"

"Who are you?" he all but growled.

She raised one thinly shaped brow. "May I ask who you are first?"

"Callan Sinclair."

She narrowed her eyes in thought, then opened them wide. "Oh, Sinclair. You must be Gabe and Lucian's brother. They own this company, but I haven't met them yet."

"We all own this company," Cal said tightly. "And your name is?"

"Francine. I'm from the employment agency."

"Where's Abigail? Is she sick?"

"Abigail?" The brunette furrowed her brow. "Oh, you mean the woman who used to work here."

"No," he said slowly and carefully. "I mean the woman who *does* work here. Blond hair, big glasses. About five-seven. Abigail Thomas."

"Oh, *her.* Right. Well, she quit," Francine chirped. "I'm her replacement."

Quit? Impossible. Abigail wouldn't quit. Cal glanced

around his office, then back at Francine. "What the hell happened here?"

Eyes wide behind a thick layer of mascara and purple eye shadow, she looked around the room. "Well, it's only my first day, for Heaven's sake. I still have to learn your filing system. It's very confusing."

The alphabet was confusing? Cal felt his skull pressing in on his brain as he waved a hand at the hanging blueprints. "And this?"

"Oh, gosh, Wayne feels awful about that."

"Wayne?"

"Cute little old gray-haired man, mustache."

"The civil engineer?"

She nodded. "I was helping him roll out the plans for one of your projects, and he sort of spilled his coffee."

Cal gritted his teeth. With the way Francine was about to fall out of her top, he was surprised Wayne hadn't had a coronary.

When he noticed that the computer screen on the desk in front of the brunette was flashing "Fatal Error, File Deleted," Cal was certain *he* was going to have a coronary.

How could this have happened in one day? Cal had spoken with Abigail only yesterday. Everything had been fine. Terrific, in fact. How could she just leave him like this? Without any notice or even a word of goodbye? She *wouldn't* do this to him.

"Do either of my brothers know about Miss Thomas leaving?" Cal asked his new, and soon-to-be-former, secretary.

Francine shook her head. "They haven't been in the office today. Miss Thomas told me that Gabe mostly works out of his house and Lucian rarely comes in here. Can I get you some coffee, Mr. Sinclair?"

Cal glanced at the coffeepot on the counter behind the woman. So *that* was what he smelled burning. With a scowl, he looked back at Francine. "Did Miss Thomas say anything to you about why she left, or where she went?"

The question seemed a difficult one for Francine. She chewed on her bright-pink bottom lip. "No, not that I can remember."

Not that she could remember? Cal clenched his jaw so tightly he thought his teeth might crack. "Are you sure?" he asked with a patience he'd offer a six-year-old.

When the woman narrowed her eyes in concentration, they seemed to disappear behind heavy black strokes of eyeliner. "No, she didn't say a word. Oh—" she brightened, and her eyes returned "—but she did ask me to tell you she left a letter on your desk."

Francine was still rattling on about something or other when Cal made a dash for his office, found the envelope sitting in the middle of his desk and ripped it open.

Dear Mr. Sinclair,
I regret to inform you that it has become necessary for me to leave my position as secretary for Sinclair Construction. I apologize that I was unable to give you proper notice. I realize that it is un-forgivable, and I can only hope that Francine will be a competent replacement.

Thank you for employing me for the past year. I enjoyed working for you.
Sincerely,
Abigail Thomas

Cal stared at the letter. It was typed and signed, neat as a pin.

That was it? I enjoyed working for you, but *hasta la vista,* baby? No reason, no explanation?

He crumpled the letter. Dammit, he'd find her and make her tell him what the hell this was all about. He'd pay her double, *triple,* her wage, if that's what she wanted. She could have more time off—not *too* much, of course—sick days, pension, car mileage. Anything.

He'd drive over to her house right now, he decided. Forget the shower, forget the beer. Forget everything. This was an emergency. He started for the door and stopped.

Where the hell did she live?

She'd worked for him a year, and he had no idea where her house was. Or apartment. She could live at a hotel for all he knew. Or with her family.

Did she have family? He wasn't certain. Dammit, dammit, how could he know so little about her?

He would start with his files. There had to be an address somewhere. He'd find her, and when he did—

The phone rang, and he snatched it off the hook in his office before that so-called secretary in the outer office could get it. "What is it?" he shouted into the phone.

"That's a fine way to answer your phone," his brother Reese said on the other end of the line.

"I've got a crisis here, what do you want?"

"Does it have anything to do with your secretary?"

Cal's hand tightened on the phone. "What do you know about my secretary?"

"Not much," Reese said. "Except that she's sitting

in a booth in my tavern about twenty feet away from me, and she seems quite determined to get herself drunk. I just thought—''

Cal slammed down the phone and headed for the door, ignoring the look of surprise on Francine's face as he rushed past her. Abigail getting drunk? Cal thought incredulously. She didn't drink. Or did she? He had no idea. She could be a raging alcoholic, for all he knew.

He'd find out soon enough, he resolved. He intended to learn everything there was to know about Miss Abigail Thomas. And then he'd bring her right back here, where she belonged.

No matter what the cost.

Abigail had never been inside Squire's Tavern and Inn before. For the past year she'd driven by the establishment every day on her way to and from work, but until today she'd never considered going in. Like its name suggested, the tavern's theme was Old English: the ceiling was open beamed; the walls were covered with dark wood paneling; the huge fireplace had been built of rugged stone. Except for the television over the bar and the Bob Seger song playing from the corner jukebox, Abigail could easily picture the restaurant-bar as a setting for a pub in one of Shakespeare's plays.

It was still early in the day, and she was thankful there were only a few other people in the tavern: a man and woman at a small table sharing a bottle of wine and three men at the bar drinking beer and eating pretzels. No one seemed to notice her, but that wasn't unusual. No one ever noticed Abigail Thomas.

And that was exactly the way she wanted it.

Taking a deep breath, Abigail sat straighter, then took a sip from the thin, red plastic straw in the drink the waitress had brought her.

And choked.

Good Lord! She felt as if she'd swallowed liquid fire. Grabbing the white paper napkin that her glass had been sitting on, she pressed it daintily to her lips and breathed through her mouth. She'd managed to reach the ripe old age of twenty-six without knowing that hard alcohol tasted so awful, and she wouldn't mind another twenty-six years without tasting it again. She'd ordered the harmless-sounding drink from a small plastic menu, and she realized now she probably should have asked the waitress what was in the mixture.

Whatever it was, it burned all the way down her throat clear to her stomach and was currently working its way to her toes. She should have ordered a glass of wine, not because she especially liked wine, but at least it didn't make her choke.

Oh, what did it matter? she thought, and held her breath this time as she took another long sip. She wasn't drinking for pleasure.

She was drinking for effect.

After several more minutes and several more sips, Abigail decided that the effect *was* pleasurable, after all, in an ethereal kind of way. She felt lighter, and the soft buzz in her head made her smile at the silliest things—like the enormous ears on one of the men sitting at the bar or the monkey playing the piano on the television set mounted on the wall. That was hilarious.

Wincing, she took another sip and shivered as it slid down her throat. Maybe before the night was through she'd find some humor in quitting her job, too.

Abigail had worried all day about the woman the

agency had sent to replace her. Francine had not been dressed appropriately, nor had she had adequate training. But she was all the agency had, and Abigail had been compelled to hire her. With Aunt Ruby and Aunt Emerald coming into town tomorrow afternoon, there was no way Abigail could stay at Sinclair Construction.

How could she face Mr. Sinclair once he found out that she'd lied? It would be too humiliating, too demoralizing.

So she'd quit. She felt awful leaving him without the proper notice, but she'd had no choice. If Francine didn't work out, he would find someone else. He'd have to.

She felt the burn of tears in her eyes and blinked them away. She couldn't allow herself to think about Mr. Callan Sinclair. She was in a public place, for Heaven's sake, and she certainly didn't want to make a spectacle of herself. She simply wanted to sit here, alone, and forget about her boss and her job and her aunts coming into town.

"Oh, what a tangled web we weave..." she thought to herself.

With a sigh she took another long sip of her drink and was surprised when it didn't taste nearly as bad as it had the first few sips. She thought it actually tasted kind of good, in fact. A little sweet, yet sour at the same time. And it made her insides feel warm.

She liked the feeling, she decided, and loosened the top button of the white blouse she had on under her brown suit jacket. For the next few hours she was determined not to think about the mess she'd made of her life.

She'd have plenty of time for that tomorrow. Or

worse—she loosened another button—for the rest of her life.

The song on the jukebox changed to a number from the musical *Grease,* the one where Olivia Newton-John's character tells John Travolta he'd "better shape up." She smiled at the song, mentally singing along with the piece she knew only too well.

In her mind Abby crushed a cigarette under her four-inch heel, pointed a finger at Travolta and wiggled her hips as she told him she needed a man to keep her satisfied. Strange that the man in her mind didn't look like Travolta, but like Mr. Sinclair.

"Mind if I join you?"

Abigail jumped, then slowly, breath held, glanced over her shoulder.

Oh, dear.

Abigail's heart started to pound as she stared up at Callan Sinclair. His dark-chocolate-brown eyes bored into her, his mouth was pressed into a tight line. He looked so serious, she thought. So somber. For some strange reason, she suddenly found that very funny.

But rather than be rude and laugh, she composed herself, straightened her glasses and simply nodded.

He slid into the seat across from her and filled the booth. Filled her senses. He looked and smelled like a man who'd marched through mud and muck, and she wondered why the earthy scent of him fascinated her so. Or why she found the gray powder covering his hair and chambray shirt so attractive. *Rugged* was the word that came to mind. And *virile.*

Normally Abigail found Callan Sinclair's presence intimidating. At six-three, his height alone was enough to make a person—man or woman—take notice. And he certainly was powerfully built, with solid muscles and a broad chest. He was also incredibly handsome, she thought, with his thick, black hair and devastating smile.

But he wasn't smiling now, she realized, and she was the reason.

He placed his large hands flat on the wood tabletop and leaned close. He had wonderful hands, she thought, staring at them. A man's hands, large and rough, with short, blunt nails and a long, jagged scar on his right thumb. She had the craziest desire to cover those hands with her own, to feel their roughness under her smooth palms.

When she lifted her eyes to his, the intensity of his dark gaze seemed to suck the air right out of her lungs. She couldn't remember ever having had his undivided attention like this or having him look at her, *really* look at her as he was looking at her right now. For the first time in the past year, she didn't feel as if she were invisible.

She wasn't certain she liked the feeling at all.

"Mr. Sinclair—"

"I refuse to accept your resignation."

His deep, familiar voice had never sounded so gruff before, so firm. *He cares about me,* she thought in amazement, then quickly chided herself. *As an employee, of course.*

She folded her hands primly in her lap and held his level gaze. "I apologize for leaving so suddenly, but I'm certain that Francine will work out for you. She's really quite—"

"I *said*—" he leaned closer, lowering his voice, but it still sounded like a shout "—I *refuse* to accept your resignation. Francine is history. I want you, Abigail."

His words thrilled her, yet flustered her at the same

time. *I want you, Abigail.* She felt herself sway toward him.

As a secretary, *you ninny,* Abigail yelled silently at herself. She blinked, then pulled back. Because she didn't know what to say, she took another long pull on her drink. It didn't burn at all now; it tasted wonderful. She realized it was nearly gone and didn't want it to be.

"May I buy you a drink, Mr. Sinclair?" She'd never bought a man a drink in her life. Except for Lester Green at the insurance company she'd worked for in New York, but that was a root beer from the soda machine, so she didn't think it counted. And Lester didn't have sexy eyes like Mr. Sinclair did. He had eyes like Eeyore.

That thought made her giggle. Her ex-boss raised one brow and looked down at the glass in front of her. "What do you have?"

"Iced tea."

"Iced tea?"

"Manhattan iced tea," she repeated and took another sip.

He coughed, then raised both brows. "You mean a Long Island iced tea?"

"That's it," she said with delight. "Would you like one?"

"Have you ever had one before?" he asked carefully.

"Of course not, silly." She clapped a hand over her mouth. "Oh, Mr. Sinclair, I'm so sorry."

"Why don't you call me Callan for right now?" he said with a sigh, then turned and made a gesture to a man standing behind the bar.

A man who looked strangely familiar, Abigail

thought, and slid her reading glasses down her nose so she could get a better look. "Do you know that man?" she asked.

"My brother Reese," he answered. "He owns this place."

Reese Sinclair. Abigail nearly groaned. He'd been in the office several times over the past year. In her discomposed state, she'd forgotten he owned Squire's Tavern. So that was how Mr. Sinclair had found her so quickly.

Darn it, darn it, *darn* it.

"Mr. Sinclair, I truly am—"

"Callan," he reminded her.

"Callan," she said awkwardly. She'd never called him by his first name. "I'm sorry for leaving your employment so suddenly. I'm afraid I had no choice."

The waitress brought a frosted mug of beer and a steaming cup of coffee, then quickly left. Callan pushed the coffee at her.

She didn't want coffee. For the first time today, her stomach wasn't in knots, and her chest wasn't aching. She felt calm and relaxed and just a little giddy.

And hot. She felt hot. She unloosened another button and, ignoring the coffee, took another sip of her drink. She still felt hot, so she slipped her jacket off.

Callan's beer sloshed over the side of his mug when she fanned the open vee of her blouse. He frowned at her and set his drink back down. "You owe me an explanation, Abigail. You can't just leave me and not even tell me why. Did you find another job?"

"No."

"Do you want more money?"

She lifted her chin at his insult. "Certainly not. If I'd wanted more money, I would have asked you."

"So why did you quit?"

"I can't tell you. It's personal."

Callan's eyes darkened with concern. "Are you sick?"

She shook her head.

"Pregnant?"

"Heavens, no!" Her eyes went wide at the absurdity of *that* question.

He thought for a minute. "You're engaged."

She blinked slowly, then her gaze dropped, and she took another sip of her drink.

"That's it?" He leaned closer, surprise on his face. "You're engaged?"

Her heart started to pound. She wanted to deny it, tell him that her being engaged was absolute nonsense, but even with alcohol rushing through her veins, she still couldn't lie.

"Something like that," she mumbled, and felt her cheeks burn.

"Something like that?" He narrowed his eyes. "Who?"

"Excuse me?" she repeated.

"Who is it?" he asked. "Bloomfield isn't all that big a town, maybe I know him."

The foolishness of her situation suddenly struck Abigail. She covered her mouth and started to laugh. Callan stared at her incredulously.

"What's so funny?" he asked.

"You are," she said between giggles.

"I'm funny?"

"No." She sucked in a breath and composed herself. "You're my fiancé."

Two

He was her fiancé?

Callan stared at her, narrowed his eyes, then stared at her some more. She'd said the words perfectly clearly, but he must have heard her wrong.

"Excuse me?"

"*You're* my fiancé." She stared down into her near-empty drink, and her glasses started to slip down her nose. She pushed them back up with her index finger and looked at him, her brow furrowed. "Don't you see that's why I had to quit? It's so humiliating."

He didn't see at all. In fact, he was completely blind on this one. It had to be the drink, he decided. She was confused. Extremely confused.

But then, so was he.

"It's humiliating to be engaged to me?" he asked.

"Of course it is."

Callan frowned at the exasperation in her voice.

What was so wrong with him that she'd be embarrassed to be engaged to him? A lot of women found him attractive, and more than one had tried to lead him on that walk down the aisle. Just because he and Abigail were so completely different and had never been attracted to each other was certainly no reason to be *humiliated.*

Oh, for crying out loud, he thought, rolling his eyes. What the hell was he thinking? They *weren't* engaged. Or anything even remotely close. He shook his head and laughed at himself, amazed that Abigail had actually managed to tweak his male pride.

He leaned back in the booth, tried not to notice that Abigail had not only removed her jacket, but had loosened three buttons. The unmistakable swell of full breasts rose from the opened blouse. Good Lord, he'd never thought about Abigail having breasts, let alone such nice ones. He reached for his beer and forced his eyes to stay steady on her flushed face.

He had to remind himself what they'd been talking about. Oh, yes. She was humiliated to be engaged to him. "Abigail, I hate to tell you this, but we're not engaged."

She laughed, then flipped her hand at him with a you're-such-a-silly-boy gesture. "Of *course* we're not. But Aunt Emerald and Aunt Ruby don't know that."

He was afraid to ask. "Aunt Emerald and Aunt Ruby?"

"They're coming to visit tomorrow, before they go on their two-week cruise in the Caribbean." The smile on her face dissolved. She leaned back in the booth and closed her eyes. "Don't you think it's hot in here?"

When Abigail reached up and opened another button

on her blouse, exposing more of her breasts and the top edge of her pale-green lace bra, Callan felt his throat turn to powder.

She was right. It *was* hot in here.

He had to get her out of here. Fast. For her sake as much as his own. Aunt Emerald and Aunt Ruby and engagements would have to wait for now.

Sliding out of the booth, he reached for the suit jacket she'd removed, then slipped a hand behind her back and pulled her toward him. Her skin was remarkably warm through her blouse, and the faint feminine scent of her perfume drifted into his senses. He'd never noticed she wore perfume before, he thought, as he tugged her jacket back on her and pulled the front tightly closed.

Her eyes opened wide. They were green, he realized. Soft green. He'd never noticed that before, either. She stared indignantly at him. "Mr. Sinclair, what *are* you doing?"

He sighed heavily. "I'm taking you home."

"That won't be necessary." She shrugged out of his hold and straightened her jacket, then peered up at him with a strange squint. "You don't look anything like John Travolta."

He had no idea how to respond to that one. "Okay."

"I just want you to know how much I enjoyed working for you, Mr. Sinclair—"

"Callan."

"Callan," she said his name softly, as if she'd never heard it before. She looked at him for a long moment, then whispered, "I'm sorry."

He could have sworn he saw tears in her eyes before she turned and wobbled away. Abigail cry? No, Callan thought. Abigail didn't cry. She was always so...so *together*.

Well, except for at the moment, anyway. He watched her teeter toward the rest rooms, then raised his brows when she walked into the men's room.

Uh-oh.

He was on his way to rescue her when she came back out of the rest room, her face bright red. Tom Winters, Bloomfield County Mayor, came out a few steps behind her. His face was red, too.

"Callan." Tom nodded stiffly and kept walking.

"Tom." Callan held back the threatening grin.

"Mr. Sinclair." Abigail put a hand on his arm and leaned against him, then said in a small voice, "Callan, could you please drive me home?"

Abigail's home was only three short blocks away: a little white cottage covered with thick vines of pink roses. Callan hadn't quite pictured Abigail in such a feminine-looking house, but then, he hadn't ever pictured her in any style house.

He pulled his truck into the narrow asphalt driveway, thankful that she'd at least been clear-headed enough to give directions. He cut the engine and climbed out, then came around and opened the door for her. She reached for her purse at the same time she stepped out, and ended up sliding off the seat into his arms. Her body pressed against his while he steadied her.

"Excuse me," she said, then hiccuped.

Damn, but Abigail was soft, Callan thought. And curvy. Damn.

She pressed a palm against his chest and pushed away from him, then straightened her glasses. Long strands of blond hair had escaped from the bun at the back of her head and tumbled around her flushed face. "Thank you for the ride home, Mr. Sinclair. Goodbye."

He watched her turn on unsteady legs and walk crookedly toward her front door. *Goodbye?* No way he was leaving. He had no intention of letting her out of his sight. Especially in her condition.

He followed her up the brick walkway, noticing that her lawn was mowed and neatly edged, her bushes trimmed and her flower beds free of weeds. She paused when she reached the step leading onto her front porch and stared at it as if it were a steep cliff.

"Abigail." He took her arm and helped her up the step. "We need to talk."

She dug through her purse. "Here they are." She pulled her keys from her purse and smiled brightly.

He took the keys from her and opened the door. "How 'bout I make us some coffee?"

She laughed at that. "*You* make coffee? I'm supposed to make the coffee, remember? That's my job." She frowned suddenly. "At least it *was* my job. Until I quit. Francine will have to make you coffee now."

Callan shuddered at the thought and ushered Abigail inside the door. The living room was cozy: the overstuffed blue-gingham sofa was accented with floral pillows; the walls were covered with various watercolor landscapes. A thick, deep-blue rug edged with pink flowers lay neatly on the shiny hardwood floor. A crystal vase filled with fragrant pink roses sat on top of an oval mahogany coffee table.

She was as tidy and organized at home as she was at work, Callan thought, but he hadn't expected all the hearts-and-flowers decor. He'd have thought her home would be more...simple. Plain.

Dull was actually the word that came to mind.

Except it wasn't dull at all, he thought. It was warm and comfortable. Homey. He realized he had a lot to learn about Abigail. A whole lot.

But he would think about the many unknown facets of Abigail Thomas later. At the moment he intended to start with the mystery of her sudden departure from his office and where their strange engagement and her aunts fit into the puzzle.

Now where had she disappeared to?

He heard the pop of a cork and followed the sound into her kitchen. Barefoot, Abigail stood at the counter, pouring white wine into a glass.

He groaned silently.

"Abigail," he said, moving behind her. "I thought we were going to have coffee."

"No-o-o-o," she said, stretching the word out as she kept pouring. Some of the wine actually made it into the glass. "*You're* going to have coffee. I'm having wine."

"You don't drink much, do you?" he asked.

She giggled at that. "Heavens, no. I don't care for the taste, and besides, it affects me terribly."

That was an understatement, he thought, then swooped the glass of wine off the counter when she started to reach for it. He took a sip. Yuck. He'd take a cold beer over white wine any day. "Thanks."

She frowned at him. "I thought you wanted coffee."

"I changed my mind." He took a second sip, tried not to grimace. She was reaching for another glass when he took her arm and led her to the kitchen table. "Abigail, you owe it to me to tell me why you quit."

Pulling out a chair, he gently eased her into it. Her skirt pulled high up on her legs when she sat, exposing smooth, slender thighs. The Abigail he knew would have quickly pulled her skirt back down. This Abigail left it to ride high on her legs. Callan glanced away and took another sip of wine, thankful that at least she still had her jacket on.

He kept his eyes riveted on her face.

She leaned her elbows on the table and covered her face with her hands. "It's so humiliating."

"We established that." He sat in the chair beside her. A fluffy, ruffled blue-striped pad covered the seat. "You and me being engaged. Why don't we start with that?"

"I don't feel well," she said from behind her hands. "Could you please get me a drink of water?"

He doubted a drink of water would help her problem, but if he was ever going to get any information out of her, Callan thought, he'd better humor her. He took a glass out of the cupboard, filled it with tap water, then set it in front of her as he sat back down.

And realized that she'd nearly emptied the glass of wine he'd so foolishly left sitting on the table.

"Abigail!"

With her hands folded primly in her lap, she straightened her shoulders and looked at him. Her glasses were tilted on her straight little nose, and the expression on her face was one of complete innocence. In a very strange way she looked kind of cute, Callan thought.

Rather than straighten her glasses, he reached over and took them off, then set them on the table. Her eyes were big and wide as she blinked at him, then hiccuped. He couldn't help but smile. "Abigail, tell me why you quit."

Her gaze dropped to her lap. "I had to. With Aunt

Ruby and Aunt Emerald coming in tomorrow, they would have found out.''

''Found out what?''

''That we're not engaged.''

''But we're *not* engaged.''

''Exactly.'' She threw a hand up in the air and breathed a sigh of relief. ''Thank goodness you understand.''

But he didn't. Not at all. ''Abigail, why do your aunts think that you and I are engaged?''

''Well, I told them we were, of course. Why else would they think such a thing?''

Well, of course. Silly me. He counted to five, then drew in a slow breath. ''And why did you tell them we were engaged?''

''What else was I supposed to do? They would have canceled their cruise, maybe even insisted on moving in with me here. I *had* to do something.''

''They would have canceled their cruise and moved in with you if we weren't engaged?'' He shook his head in confusion. ''Why?''

Leaning in close to him, she whispered, ''They think I need a man.''

Ah. He almost—just almost—thought he was beginning to understand. ''They do?''

She nodded. ''We lived together for two years in New York after I finished college, but it got so bad I finally moved here to Bloomfield County.''

He saw her eyeing the wineglass in front of him, and he scooted it out of her reach. ''What got so bad?''

''The men. Every week they'd bring home their latest catch for me. Sometimes if my aunts didn't coordinate, there would be *two* men at the same time.'' She held up two fingers to emphasize, and her eyes crossed as she stared at them. "Imagine every time you turned around there were women all over the place. How would you feel?"

He thought about that for a moment and decided she really didn't want an answer to that question. "Why can't you just tell your aunts the truth?"

She snorted in laughter, then covered her mouth. "You don't know my aunts. They've been mother hens since my own mother—their sister—died six years ago. They won't rest until I'm married and have a family of my own. The only reason they've left me alone so long was because of you."

"Me?"

"Our engagement."

"Oh, yes." He'd nearly forgotten about that. "And how did you happen to pick me to be the lucky guy?"

"Well, I had to have *someone,*" she said as if he'd missed the obvious. "I don't know anyone else here."

How flattering to know he'd been chosen because there wasn't anyone else. "You could have made someone up," he suggested.

"That would be a big lie. I'm not good with big lies. There's too much to remember, and I always trip myself up. I'm much better with little lies."

He didn't exactly think that Abigail telling her aunts they were engaged was a "little" lie, but that wasn't important right now. Getting her back to work for him was.

"You could have told me this, Abigail." Callan took her hands in his. He was amazed at how soft and warm they were. "We would have figured something out."

She stared down at their joined hands. "You think I'm pathetic."

Oh, no, Callan groaned inwardly. The feminine mind

sober was a perilous thing, but on a Long Island iced tea, it was downright dangerous. The only thing more dangerous could be his response. "Of course I don't think you're pathetic."

"Yes, you do." She yanked her hands from his and stood, though unsteadily. "You think I'm a pathetic prude."

Shoulders squared, she moved past him. She was halfway through her living room when he caught her arm and turned her around to face him. "Abigail, please—"

She shrugged off his hand. "For your information, Mr. Sinclair, if I really wanted a man, I could find one. I'm not as big a prude as you think I am."

"Abigail, I don't—"

She tugged off her jacket and threw it on the floor. "I have a nice enough body." She reached for the buttons on her already-half-opened blouse.

"Abigail—"

"See?" She opened her blouse and stared down at herself. Her mint-green bra was lace and satin. "They aren't so bad."

So bad? His blood shot to his head, then straight down below his waist. Good Lord, she was beautiful. He was only human, for God's sake. He stared wide-eyed for a full two seconds, then closed his open mouth and pulled the front of her blouse together. His hands were shaking as he closed the top button.

She slumped against him. "Who am I trying to kid?" she said softly, closing her eyes. "I *am* a prude. I've always been a prude. I'll always *be* a prude. Abigail Thomas, Queen of the Prudes."

With a sigh, Callan cupped her chin in his hands and

lifted her face to his. "Abigail, I don't think you're a prude."

Her eyes, glazed-green, opened slowly. "You don't?"

She looked at him, her cheeks flushed, her lips wide and lush. How could he have never noticed those lips before? he thought. They were incredible. He felt a strange kick in his pulse as he stared down at her. Her skin was pale against his, so smooth and soft. When her eyes closed and her lips parted ever so slightly, he found himself drawn downward, closer…closer…

Good Lord!

He pulled back. This was *Abigail,* for Heaven's sake. He couldn't kiss Abigail.

It had to be the stress of her quitting and his exhaustion from working all day, Callan decided. He wasn't firing on all his cylinders at the moment. Abigail was his *secretary,* or at least, she *had* been his secretary. Which reminded him why he was here in the first place.

He wanted her back.

"Abigail."

"Hmm?" she murmured, her eyes still closed.

"We need to talk."

"You want to talk?" Her eyes fluttered open again.

When she swayed against him, he walked her to the sofa and pulled her down onto the soft cushions. He was too dirty to sit, but when he spotted a cotton afghan on the arm of the couch, he spread it out, then sat down on top of it.

"I need you, Abigail," he said gently.

She looked at him, then blinked. "You do?"

"You're the best secretary I ever had. I don't want to lose you."

"Oh. I see." She laid her head back on the sofa and closed her eyes again. "I'm sorry, Mr. Sinclair, but I can't come back. I just can't."

Callan watched Abigail's head drift to the side. He would let her rest for a few minutes, he decided, then they'd finish this conversation. Before this night was over, she'd say yes. He was certain of that.

He wasn't about to let her go. Whatever it took, Callan intended to have Miss Abigail Thomas back where she belonged.

Abigail woke slowly. She couldn't imagine where the cotton in her mouth had come from. Or the subtle pounding in her temple. That was odd, as well. But certainly not as odd as the steady heartbeat she heard rising from her pillow.

Eyes closed, she listened for a moment. There it was, as loud as if she were listening through a stethoscope. *Ba- bump…ba-bump…ba-bump…* Deep and steady, it pounded in her ear.

She felt a little stiff and sore, and though it took a moment for her eyes to register the command from her foggy brain, they opened slowly. Blue cotton and white buttons stared back at her.

What in the world?

That's when she heard the voices. Soft whispers. They seemed very distant, and distinctly familiar.

"He's a handsome one, don't you think?"

"Oh, dear me, yes. He looks a lot like Emmett, my leading man from *Oklahoma*. Heavens, that must have been twenty years ago."

"His name was Ethan, it was thirty years ago, and they don't look anything alike. This young man is much more handsome, though he does look a little ragged around the edges. Oh, look, I do believe our Sleeping Beauty is waking up. She has one eye open.''

This has to be a dream, Abigail thought. *Dear God, please let it be a dream.* Breath held, she opened both eyes.

And slammed them shut again.

She was on the sofa, lying across Mr. Sinclair's chest. Her blouse was open.

No, no, no, no, no.

''Good morning, Abby, dear,'' Aunt Emerald and Aunt Ruby bubbled at the same time.

Three

They stood beside each other, the quintessential *Mutt and Jeff,* and smiled down at her. Ruby was the taller of the two, with curly, tomato-red hair she always wore swept up, robust blue eyes and a thunderous voice that could set off a car alarm. Emerald was a pageboy platinum-blonde with big green eyes that always looked surprised and a generous smile that stretched wide across her pale, yet remarkably young-looking face. They were both dressed in a kaleidoscope of bright flowing gauze and dozens of matching plastic bracelets.

Eyes now wide open, Abigail stared at her aunts, then lifted her head and looked at the man whose arms were wrapped around her. Her heart slammed in her chest. She vaguely remembered sitting on the sofa with him last night, but she had no idea how she'd ended up here in his arms. In his *arms,* for Heaven's sake! Thank God he was still sleeping, she thought, and carefully tried to slip under his embrace. He mumbled softly and tightened his hold.

She bit back the groan hovering in her throat and gave her aunts a weak smile. They smiled back brightly.

With her dignity long past the point of resurrection, Abigail wiggled gently and eased herself, inch by inch, out from under her boss's—*ex*-boss's, she reminded herself—arms. She'd nearly escaped when he gave a soft snort, then opened his eyes. He stared at her in surprise, then glanced at Ruby and Emerald.

"Good morning," her aunts boomed in unison.

With a look of panic, he catapulted from the couch. Caught off balance, Abigail tumbled to the floor.

"Oh, dear." Emerald pressed a hand to her chest.

"Heavens." Ruby frowned.

Callan dragged a hand through his rumpled hair, then his gaze shifted from the two startled women back down to Abigail.

"Sorry," he said awkwardly, offering Abigail a hand. Her blouse fell open as he pulled her to her feet. He paled, then turned red. *He's blushing,* Abigail thought in amazement and quickly pulled her blouse closed. Mr. Sinclair was actually embarrassed.

And as she remembered *why* her blouse was open, she felt her own cheeks burn. *Ohmigod,* she thought with a silent groan. The memory of her near strip-tease sucked the breath from her lungs. Quickly she buttoned her blouse, desperately wishing that the sofa would open up and swallow her whole.

But she would deal with what happened last night later. First she had her aunts to contend with.

"Aunt Emerald, Aunt Ruby." Abigail's voice cracked. She straightened the front of her misbuttoned blouse, then cleared her throat. "What are you doing here?"

"We told you we were coming, dear," Ruby said, though her gaze was still locked on Callan. "Have you forgotten?"

Abigail glanced at her wristwatch. "It's only seven-thirty in the morning. I was supposed to pick you up at the airport this afternoon at one-thirty. Flight 312, Gate 22."

"Oh, that." Emerald waved a hand of dismissal. "We took an earlier flight. Ruby was supposed to tell you."

"I was not." Bracelets clacked loudly as Ruby jammed her hands on her well-endowed hips and frowned at her sister. "You were supposed to. I called for the taxi."

"You're arguing again, Ruby." Forever smiling, Emerald faced her sister and waved a finger at her, which also set her own bracelets clacking.

Great, Abigail thought. *Just what I need right now— dueling bracelets.*

"It doesn't matter," Abigail interjected before the discussion could escalate. And knowing her aunts, it most certainly would. Awkwardly she leaned forward and hugged each of them. "It's...it's wonderful to see you."

In spite of the situation, Abigail was surprised that she actually meant it. Her aunts might be eccentric and flamboyant, but she loved them both. They cooed over her, smoothed her hair and kissed her cheek, then glanced at the man whose arms she'd been in less than five minutes ago.

Abigail drew in a deep breath, then said in a rush, "Aunt Emerald, Aunt Ruby, this is Mr. Sinclair."

Two sets of confused eyes looked back at her. "Mr. Sinclair?"

"My employer." As delicately as possible she blew a strand of hair out of her eyes. "I believe I told you about him."

"You call your fiancé Mr. Sinclair?" Ruby asked.

She bit the inside of her lip. Time to face the piper. She sucked in another deep breath. "He's not—"

"—Mr. Sinclair to you lovely ladies, of course," he said smoothly. "It's Callan."

Breath held, Abigail watched as he moved beside her and casually slipped an arm around her shoulders. He took her chin between his thumb and forefinger and gave her a pinch. "Sometimes Abby can be such a tease."

Shocked, Abigail stared up at "Callan." He'd called her "Abby" and said she was a "tease?" She had to be having a hallucination. Some bizarre aftermath of too much alcohol. But when he squeezed her shoulder, he certainly didn't feel like a hallucination. He felt strong and solid.

"Abby's told me so much about you both," he went on. "I realize how strange this must look, finding us like this, but the truth is, we were up so late last night talking about your visit, we fell asleep right here. Isn't that right, Abby?"

Well, *technically* his explanation was correct, Abigail supposed, and looked back at her aunts. They beamed with pleasure.

She smiled weakly at them and shifted from one bare foot to the other. Obviously, part of taking off her clothes had included her shoes. "Well, actually, Aunties, the truth is—"

"The truth is," Callan said, interrupting again, then

paused and leaned toward her aunts as he whispered, "Abby had a little too much to drink last night. She never could hold her alcohol very well, you know."

Emerald and Ruby glanced at each other and nodded compassionately, then Ruby said, "It's a recessive gene in her father's side of the family, I'm afraid. The Bliss side of the family is quite tolerant of the spirits, though we only partake on special occasions, of course, and even then with the utmost discretion."

Abigail choked back a laugh. Discretion was hardly a word that was used synonymously with the Bliss name, and as far as special occasions, the sun rising and setting every day would most likely be considered special to her aunts. But it certainly was true that they were able to consume endless amounts of liquor without any of the side effects that plagued most people, including herself.

Especially herself, Abigail thought as the memory of the previous night began to emerge all too vividly in her mind.

She'd shown him her *breasts,* for Heaven's sake. What he must think of her, exposing herself like that to him. How could she ever face him again?

She couldn't. She just couldn't.

But at the moment, however, it seemed as though she had no choice. He still had his arm looped possessively around her shoulder and held her snugly against his broad chest. The heat of his body shimmered through his shirt and radiated through her body all the way down to her bare toes.

"Well?" Ruby's gaze dropped to her hand, and Emerald leaned forward expectantly. "Let's see it, dear."

"See it?" Abby had no idea what her aunts were talking about. "See what?"

"Why, your ring, of course," Emerald said. "We've been so excited ever since we heard the good news."

"Oh, Aunties, I'm so sorry, but—"

"—we just haven't found the right one yet," Callan finished for her. He gave her shoulder a big squeeze. "Something that important has to be perfect, don't you think?"

Startled, Abby stared up at Callan. What in the world was he talking about?

"Absolutely." Emerald gave an approving nod. "Mustn't rush things like that and be sorry for it later."

Ruby's expression was thoughtful. "Well, you know, Em, your second marriage with Artemus was rather hasty, may he rest in peace, but you have a lovely two-karat solitaire to remember him by."

"Not nearly as lovely as that three-karat cluster your third husband gave you," Emerald replied. "That puppy was the size of a Volkswagen, bless the man's heart."

They smiled in fond remembrance, sighed, then quickly turned their attention back to Abby and Callan.

"We've love to stay and chat, dear," Emerald said, and gave her niece a pat on the cheek, "but the taxi is waiting. We'll call you when we get settled in town."

"You aren't staying with me?" Abigail asked incredulously.

"Of course not." Ruby batted her eyes at Callan. "We wouldn't dream of imposing."

Since when? Abigail wondered. Her aunts loved to impose. And the one time she *wanted* them to, they weren't? "But—"

"Don't you worry about us, darling." Emerald slipped her arm through Ruby's. "We have rooms at a quaint little place in town. Squire's Tavern and Inn.

The travel agent said that the accommodations and food there are five-star.''

Abigail wasn't sure about the accommodations or food, but she could personally vouch that the drinks there were at least five-star. She was currently seeing dozens of stars from the drink she'd had there last night.

She groaned silently, remembering that Reese Sinclair owned the inn. It would only be a matter of time before her aunts learned the truth, and Abigail Thomas would be the laughingstock of Bloomfield County. *I'll change my name. Move to a small mountain town. Dye my hair and have plastic surgery.*

Gauze flowing, her aunts were halfway to the door when Ruby called over her shoulder, ''We insist you both join us at the tavern for lunch. One o'clock sharp, dears. Emmy and I can't wait to hear all the details of how you two got together.''

''Aunties, wait.'' Abigail slipped out from under the arm Mr. Sinclair had draped around her shoulders and started after her aunts, but he caught hold of her hand and held her beside him.

''We'll be there,'' he said cheerfully and waved.

Bracelets clacking, Emerald and Ruby waved back, then exited the room with all the grace and grandeur of royalty.

Abigail closed her eyes, praying this was all a nightmare that she could now awaken from, and her boring little life could go right back to boring. She slowly opened her eyes.

Mr. Sinclair's face was no more than a foot from hers, and the hint of a smile touched his lips. She sucked in a breath as she stared at that mouth. It was much too close to her own.

"There," he said casually. "That wasn't so bad, now, was it?"

"Wasn't so bad?" Moaning, she pulled her hand away from his and sank down on the couch. "I didn't tell them the truth about us, and now we're supposed to meet them for lunch? In a public place? That happens to be my definition of *bad*, Mr. Sinclair. *Very bad*."

She fell sideways and covered her head with a floral, fringed throw pillow.

"Abby, first of all, if we're going to pull this off, you're going to have to stop calling me Mr. Sinclair. And you're certainly going to have to loosen up a little. You stiffen up like a board every time I get close to you."

"Pull what off?" she said into the pillow. "And what do you mean, I stiffen up? I do not."

"Yes, you do," he replied. "Now sit up."

She shook her head, then felt the couch dip as he sat beside her. Well, maybe she *did* stiffen up just a little, she thought, and buried her head deeper under the pillow. "Please go away."

"I'm not going away." His finger brushed her cheek when he parted the fringe covering her face. "I'm going to sit right here until you talk to me."

"I can't." She tried to ignore the feel of his callused finger on her cheek and the shiver working its way up her spine. "After what I did last night, I can't ever talk to, or even look at you, again. In fact, I'm moving to Alaska."

He chuckled. "And what exactly is it that you think you did?"

Still refusing to look at him, she held up her hand and extended her index finger. "One, I told my aunts

that you were my fiancé. Two—'' her second finger
came up ''—I got drunk. Three, I...I—''

She groaned into the pillow. Oh, God. She couldn't
even *say* she'd nearly stripped for him, let alone believe she'd actually *done* it.

''Abby.'' He said her name softly, then took hold of
her shoulders and pulled her upright. When she kept
the pillow pressed to her face, he tugged it away from
her. ''It's okay to let loose once in a while. You didn't
do anything to be embarrassed about.''

''Easy for you to say.'' She still refused to look at
him. ''You weren't the one who made an idiot out of
yourself.''

Her pulse jumped when he put a finger under her
chin and tilted her face up. A midnight shadow of beard
covered the lower portion of his face, and one thick
shock of dark hair fell over his forehead. The rough
texture of his finger under her chin sent an army of tiny
shivers marching through her.

''You didn't make an idiot out of yourself,'' he said
gently. ''Actually you were kind of cute.''

''*Cute?*'' She blinked at him. ''Mr. Sinclair, please
don't patronize or lie to me.''

He shook his head. ''I'm not lying or patronizing.
Now say my name.''

''Mr. Sinclair?''

''Callan, or Cal, if you prefer.''

''Why?''

He sighed. ''You want your aunts to go on their trip
and not move in with you, right?''

''Well, yes, I—''

''Then I'm your man.''

''What?''

"You told me that your aunts think you need a man, right?"

She felt her cheeks burn. "Well, I suppose I may have said—"

"So for the two weeks your aunts are here, I'm your man, Abby."

"You're my man?" she whispered.

He nodded. "For two whole weeks, I'm all yours."

Abigail suddenly found it hard to breathe, let alone speak. Her mind felt sluggish and heavy, but she knew it had nothing to do with the alcohol she'd consumed last night and everything to do with the touch of Callan's finger on her chin and the way he'd said, "I'm all yours."

She shook her head. "I don't understand."

"I want you back, Abigail," he said firmly. "And if that means pretending to be your fiancé for a few days, then fine. We'll make your aunts happy, and after they leave, everything will go back to normal."

Normal? He actually thought that they could pretend to be engaged, and after her aunts left, they could go back to *normal?* She didn't believe that for a moment. This was a very dangerous proposition he was making her. She'd be a fool to accept. A complete and utter fool.

She couldn't do it. She couldn't.

Could she?

"My aunts will never believe it," she said, though her voice sounded as if it belonged to someone else.

"Well, we'll just have to be convincing, then, won't we?" he murmured. "Now say my name."

She swallowed hard, then squeaked, "Callan."

He rolled his eyes. "You sound like Minnie Mouse. Try it again."

She looked at his mouth again, felt her own lips tingle. "Callan," she breathed.

His gaze dropped to her mouth, and before he released her, she could swear his thumb brushed over her jaw. Still staring at her mouth, he cleared his throat. "Well, there. Now, that wasn't so hard, was it?"

No, she thought with a sense of dread. It wasn't hard at all. In fact, it was much too easy.

He rose suddenly, still looking at her as he tripped over the leg of her coffee table. "You don't need to come in to the office this morning. I'll, ah, meet you at the tavern at one o'clock."

"But—"

"One o'clock," he backed toward the front door, then closed it behind him on his way out.

This was a bad idea, she thought and stared at the door. Bad, bad idea. They would never get away with it.

Closing her eyes, she realized that she hadn't even warned him about her aunts and their...unpredictable behavior. Unless Emerald and Ruby were unusually subdued, which Abby seriously doubted, Callan Sinclair was in for a lunch he'd never forget.

With a gasp she opened her eyes abruptly.

Oh, no.

There was one other little minor detail she'd forgotten to mention. Only it wasn't exactly minor, and it certainly wasn't little.

Groaning, she slumped back on the couch and realized the full meaning of jumping from the frying pan into the fire.

"You want me to pretend you're *what?*" Standing behind the bar, Reese Sinclair looked up sharply from the beer mug he was busy filling. "To *who?*"

"Keep it down, will you?" Callan frowned at his brother, then quickly glanced over his shoulder at Abby and her aunts sitting at a table in the middle of the tavern. The lunch crowd was heavy today, and neither Abby nor her aunts had spotted him yet. "Engaged. I want you to pretend I'm engaged. To Abby."

Beer poured over the sides of the frosty mug in Reese's hand. He swore, then reached for a towel. "You're kidding, right? You and...Abby? Since when do you call Abigail *Abby?*"

He'd decided that if they were going to be "engaged" he should think of her as Abby. "Since this morning."

"This morning?" Reese raised both brows. "You mean *morning,* as in, woke up next to her?"

"Something like that." He'd actually woken up *under* her, he recalled and remembered the feel of her soft, slender body on top of his. Strange, but he could still feel the warmth of her skin on his chest and the brush of her silky hair against his face.

Reese slung the towel over his shoulder and narrowed his eyes. "She was a little tipsy when she left here with you last night. If you're trying to string her along to ease a guilty conscience, I'm not having any part of it."

"Reese, for God's sake, will you—"

"Abigail's a nice girl," Reese went on. "A little dull, maybe, but sweet. I wouldn't like to think that my own brother took advantage of a kid like that."

Kid? Abby was no kid, Cal thought, remembering the womanly curves she'd been so insistent on showing him last night. And under different circumstances, with any other woman, he would have been more than eager to see that incredible body. But this was Abby, for God's sake. He couldn't think that way about Abby.

"She's twenty-six, for your information," Cal said irritably. "And no, I didn't take advantage of her, you moron. We fell asleep on the couch, with our clothes on, that's all."

Well, maybe there was a little more than that, but whatever happened last night was between him and Abby, Callan thought, then glanced over at the table again. As if she knew he was watching her, she slowly looked up and met his gaze.

He felt an odd catch in his throat as he stared back at her. She wore a high-collared gray sweater, and he realized it was the first time he'd seen her without a business suit—well, other than last night, but she had been wearing her suit then, too, or at least *most* of it. He looked at the oversize sweater she had on, the big, black-rimmed glasses, the tight knot of blond hair at the base of her neck, and he wondered why all this time she'd been hiding behind a facade of plain, when she really wasn't plain at all. She was actually kind of pretty. More than *kind of,* he thought. She had really soft, smooth skin, her eyes were an unusual shade of gray-green, and that body, well, hot damn, that body was—

"Cal, hello, anybody home?" Reese waved a hand in front of his face and pulled him out of his illicit thoughts. "What's the matter with you?"

Hell if he knew. Scrubbing a hand over his face, Callan dragged his gaze from Abby's back to his brother's. "See those two women sitting with Abby?"

Reese glanced over and nodded. "The Bliss sisters. I checked them into their rooms this morning."

"Those are Abby's aunts," Callan said. "If they say anything about her and me getting married, just go along with it. I'll explain later."

Emerald suddenly caught sight of Cal and, smiling that Cheshire Cat grin of hers, she waved wildly and yoo-hooed. Ruby joined in, and together they were more than loud enough to be heard over the din of conversation and the Rod Stewart song blaring from the jukebox. And though the song kept playing, conversation in the restaurant all but halted.

Every eye in the place was directed at him.

Sucking in a deep breath, he forced a smile, then made his way to the table, certain he heard his brother chuckling behind him.

Callan clenched his jaw. How dare his own brother laugh at him? Couldn't he see this was a serious situation? One that called for discretion and reserve? At thirty-one, and the youngest Sinclair male, Reese obviously needed to be taught a little more respect for his elders. Callan decided that he'd punch his lights out later. His brothers Lucian and Gabe and certainly Cara, his sister and the youngest of the Sinclair clan, would have a little more sympathy and be a lot more mature about this.

But dammit, anyway, what else could he do? Callan thought. He couldn't let Abby leave him. How could he bring another woman into his office? Abby was essential to the smooth operation of his business. And after five minutes with Francine…well, shoot, he'd rather walk naked through a blackberry bush than have that woman in his office.

For two weeks all he and Abby had to do was act engaged. Hold hands, give a little kiss here and there, a few longing looks. How hard could that be? Both he and Abby would know it wasn't real. That it was just an act.

He had to admit, though, that for a moment this morning, when he'd been sitting next to Abby on the sofa and her eyes had gone all soft when he'd touched her chin, he'd felt…well, attracted. Maybe even a little…turned on.

Okay, maybe a lot turned on.

That's why he'd hightailed it out of there. He was just having a momentary lapse of control, for lack of a better word. He didn't want Abby to get the wrong idea about his intentions, or think that he'd try to take advantage of the situation. All he wanted was her back in his office, where she belonged. Once Emerald and Ruby were convinced that he and Abby were in love, then they could go on their cruise, and later Abby could tell them that they'd broken off their engagement due to…irreconcilable differences. That would give Abby a little more time to really find a man.

And then everyone would be happy.

Pleased with himself and his simple solution, Callan ignored the curious stares from the room and pulled out the wooden chair beside Abby. Her cheeks were flushed, her brow furrowed as she glanced up at him. When he slipped an arm around her and kissed her warm cheek, he felt her sudden intake of breath.

He nodded hello to Emerald and Ruby, then murmured to Abby, "Hello, darling."

Wide-eyed, she stared at him, then hesitantly replied, "Uh, hello."

Callan sighed silently. They were definitely going to have to work on loosening Abby up, or her aunts were never going to believe they were engaged. He took her hand in his and kissed her fingers. They were cold as icicles. "I missed you."

She smiled nervously. "I, uh, missed you, too."

"You know, darling," he said, rubbing her knuckles against his chin, "I thought about our conversation this morning, about rings, and I decided I couldn't wait any longer."

Abby's eyes widened as he pulled a sparkling diamond ring out of his pocket and slipped it on her finger.

On a small sob, Emerald grabbed Ruby's arm. "Oh, Ruby, if only our dear sister could have been here to see this. Our little Abby, all grown-up and in love."

"It's a dream come true." Ruby pulled a handkerchief from her pocket and dabbed at her eyes.

"Yes, a dream come true," Emerald repeated. They looked at each other, smiled, then nodded.

Abby jerked her gaze from the ring on her finger and leaned anxiously toward her aunts. "No, Aunties, please, not now—"

The song exploded from the two women at the same time. Like a cannonball, loud and booming, something familiar about love and dreams, but Callan was too stunned to play Name That Tune. All he could do was stare.

Which was what the rest of the people in the restaurant were doing, as well.

Emerald was soprano, Ruby alto. Their voices blended beautifully, clear and strong. They continued for two stanzas, finished off with a chorus, then settled back in their chairs as calmly as if they'd just asked the waiter for more water.

The crowd broke into applause. Emerald and Ruby both stood and bowed, then reseated themselves with the grace of debutantes.

What the hell?

Callan looked at Abby, who was bright red. She had a vise-like grip on his hand.

"Oh, dear, I believe we've embarrassed Abby," Ruby said thoughtfully. "She never was comfortable with our spontaneous performances."

"Nonsense." Emerald gave her hand a shake of dismissal. "With four generations in the theater on her mother's side and three on her father's, how could she possibly be embarrassed? It's in her blood."

Abby's family in the theater? Well, that certainly explained a lot of things, Callan thought. Or did it? He wasn't so sure. "Well, that was certainly—" he struggled for the right word "—amazing."

"A mere pittance of our repertoire," Ruby announced. "But we'll save the rest for another time. Right now Emerald and I want to hear every teensy-weensy, itsy-bitsy detail about you two. You start, Callan. When was the first time that you knew our little Abby was the woman for you?"

The sisters leaned forward, their faces anxious and waiting.

The chair Callan was sitting on suddenly felt extremely warm. Pretending to be Abby's fiancé was one thing, but making up stories about how they fell in love—when of course they hadn't—was an entirely different matter.

"Mr.—" Abby caught herself, then said awkwardly, "Callan, you don't have to—"

He thought of Francine and shuddered, then slipped an arm around Abby's stiff shoulders and smiled at Emerald and Ruby. "But I *do* have to, darling. I *want* to." He leaned closer to Abby's aunts and lowered his voice. "I never told Abby this, but I knew she was the woman for me before I even laid eyes on her."

Emerald laid a hand on her ample bosom. "A premonition?"

Ruby's eyes widened. "A dream?"

"Definitely a dream." Callan remembered Abby's résumé: neatly typed, lots of office experience, could start immediately and willing to work overtime. Amidst a nightmare sea of "Francines," Abby had truly been a dream come true.

Ruby and Emerald looked at each other and sighed. "Now your turn, Abby, dear," Emerald encouraged.

"Ah..." Abby had the deer-caught-in-headlights look in her eyes as she stared at her aunts. "Well..."

Callan gave her shoulder a reassuring hug. "Don't be shy, sweetheart. Go ahead. When was the first time you knew I was the one?"

She hesitated for several seconds, then her gaze lifted to his slowly and held.

"The first time I saw you," she said quietly. "You were standing by the copier in your office, with ink all over your hands from the cartridge you'd just changed and a big black smudge on your chin. That's when I knew."

Something caught in Callan's throat as he stared at Abby. Damn, but that theatrical ability obviously *was* in Abby's blood. For one wild moment, *he* almost believed her.

He swallowed hard, then, to make the illusion complete, pressed a kiss to her lips.

Her soft, warm lips.

Just to make it look good, he held the kiss, lingered over her mouth, breathed in the sweet feminine scent that was Abby. He felt her lips tremble under his...

Callan jumped at the new and unexpected burst of song as Emerald and Ruby began to sing "Some Enchanted Evening." His heart pounding, he stared at the women, then looked at Abby. Her eyes were wide, her expression apologetic as she stared back at him.

Cheers and applause persuaded Abby's aunts to continue, which they enthusiastically did.

Bemused, Callan waited for his pulse to settle. It wasn't the kiss that had rattled him, he told himself. Hell, that little peck he'd given Abby could hardly be considered a kiss. It was simply her aunts' bizarre behavior, that's all.

Nevertheless, as Callan sat back and waited for Emerald and Ruby to finish their song, he wondered what the hell he'd gotten himself into.

Four

Abby stared at the pile of mail flowing over her desk, the blueprints strung from one doorway to the other and the mountains of files scattered on the small sofa and coffee table that made up the waiting room area. She'd only been gone from her desk since yesterday afternoon and already the office was almost as big a mess as her life.

Almost, but not quite.

With a sigh she closed the office door behind her and made her way to her desk, stepping around several boxes lying in the middle of the floor. Callan's office door was ajar, and she could hear him talking on the phone.

"No, Ray, Abigail hasn't left. Francine was just filling in for the day." Pause. "Damn right. I agree completely. No one could take Abigail's place here."

Abby hesitated, feeling a little guilty over eaves-

dropping, but too curious not to listen. The Ray who
Callan was talking to had to be Ray Palmer, a devel-
oper from Boston who was building a new shopping
center and movie theater in Bloomfield. He was a demanding, oftentimes difficult man, and though Abby
had never met the man in person, she'd enjoyed working with him in spite of his gruff manner. Maybe it
had been the flowers he'd sent her one day after losing
his temper on the phone over a permit problem, or
maybe it was simply the way he always asked her how
she was, as if he really cared. He was a lonely widower
with a grown "single" son whom he'd mentioned several times to her with the obvious intention of match-
making.

"Don't worry, Ray," Callan went on. "Abigail's not
going anywhere. She's much too valuable to Sinclair
Construction to ever let go."

Abby had to swallow the lump in her throat. Knowing that she was "valuable to Sinclair Construction"
should make her feel proud and happy. So why did she
feel as though she wanted to cry?

She was just a little overwhelmed at the moment,
that was all. Why wouldn't she feel a little emotional?
In the past twenty-four hours, she'd quit her job,
flashed her breasts at her boss, and gotten "engaged."
The same old things that every woman went through
on a daily basis.

She had to leave. She'd thought she could face him,
talk to him, but she couldn't. Not now, at least. Not
with the feel of that kiss he'd so gently, and so casually, planted on her during lunch. Her mouth still tingled from the touch of his lips on hers, For that matter,
her entire body tingled. How could she have a conversation with him with that image so strong in her mind?

And when he'd slipped that ring on her finger, she'd felt as if an electrical current had shimmered up her arm. She lifted her hand and stared at the ring now, felt that same jolt of electricity rush through her blood.

"Abby?"

She jumped at the sound of his voice. Breath held, she looked over her shoulder and saw him watching her from his doorway. She hadn't even realized that he'd hung up the phone.

Darn, darn, darn. She turned slowly and faced him. "Oh, hello."

He glanced behind her. "I thought you were taking your aunts sight-seeing."

"I told them I had something important to do at the office." Not wanting to look directly at him, she focused on her computer screen, felt her pulse jump at the "Fatal Error" message on the monitor. Oh, dear. "They dropped me off here, then took my car and headed for the theater district in Philadelphia."

He had an amused look in his eyes as he folded his arms and leaned against the doorjamb of his office. "Is there anyone we need to warn?"

"The entire city, most likely." Needing to keep busy, she picked up a manila folder sitting on the sofa, straightened the papers inside, then moved to the file cabinet beside her desk. "But if they keep to the route I mapped out for them, they shouldn't get into too much trouble."

Callan chuckled. "Something tells me your aunts aren't the kind of people who pay a lot of attention to maps."

"I suppose they aren't." She could picture them now, driving down a dirt road that was just too tempt-

ing to pass by. They would probably end up in a cow
pasture somewhere, or in an Amish barn.

Closing the file cabinet with a soft click, Abby
turned and faced Callan. "Mr. Sinclair, about this
ring…" She gently touched the gold band. "Well, you
shouldn't have gone to so much trouble. I insist on
reimbursing you for your expense."

"Not necessary," he said, glancing at the ring. "It
has a fourteen-day return policy. Do you like it?"

"It's beautiful." Exactly what she would have chosen herself, she thought. Her gaze lingered on the bril-
liant diamond and shiny gold band, and the lump that
had been in her throat a few moments ago felt as if it
had moved to her chest.

No one had ever given her anything this exquisite,
and it didn't seem to matter to her emotions that it
wasn't truly an engagement ring. She turned quickly
and blinked away the moisture burning her eyes.

"Thank you," she said softly. "For the ring and for
lunch today. I know how awkward it had to be."

He grinned at her. "*Interesting* would have been the
word I would have used."

Here it comes, she thought, and prepared herself.
From the age of six, Abby had heard the taunts and
insults about her unusual family. She'd learned to ignore the ridicule, had even pretended it didn't bother
her. But the fact was, it had hurt. It still did.

She'd spent her childhood praying that no one would
notice her, that just one day she could walk home without someone pointing a finger and laughing. Bloomfield was the first place that she'd ever felt she'd finally
fit in, the first place where no one made fun of her or
her family.

Until today. After that lunch and her aunts' musical

presentation, everyone in town would be laughing at her, talking behind her back.

Well, too bad, she thought, and lifted her chin. Let them talk. In spite of the embarrassment she'd lived with growing up, she loved her aunts.

She wasn't going to let anyone, not even Mr. Sinclair, say anything bad about Aunt Ruby or Emerald.

"I apologize if my aunts caused you any embarrassment," she said evenly. "I assure you it won't happen again."

"Did I say they embarrassed me?" He placed a hand on his chest and lifted both brows. "Of course, you might have prepared me that they break into song at the drop of a hat, but other than that tiny little quirk, I think they're terrific. Reese thought so, too. Thanks to their musical performances, his lunch crowd stayed longer and ordered more food and drink than ever. He already invited them both back for dinner, no charge, as long as they sing."

Abby groaned silently. It wouldn't be long before every one in Bloomfield heard about Ruby and Emerald Bliss, which meant that it wouldn't be long before the entire town heard about Callan Sinclair and Abigail Thomas being engaged.

Alaska wasn't far enough, she decided. A remote island somewhere. Just as long as no one knew her.

She moved to her desk and stared blankly at her computer screen. The "Fatal Error" message was definitely a sign. "This isn't going to work."

He stepped behind her and looked at the computer. "I'll get a repairman out here. Hell, I'll buy you a whole new computer if you want one."

She shook her head. "That's not what I mean. I mean you and me, pretending to be engaged. The whole town is going to hear. I can't ask you to do that.''

''You didn't ask me to do anything, Abby. This was my idea, remember? Look, we got through lunch, didn't we? We can manage a few more days.''

A few more days? How could she manage a few more days, when she'd barely made it through one little lunch? Even now his closeness made her feel light-headed. Made her feel warm. ''Mr. Sinclair—''

With a sigh, he took hold of her shoulders and turned her to face him. ''Abby, that's the first area we need to work on. Now, try it again. What's my name?''

With him holding her so close and his dark gaze so intent on her face, Abby couldn't think of her own name. *His name...*

''Callan,'' she said softly, and when he smiled his approval, she said it again, even softer, ''Callan.''

His smile faded as he stared down at her. He moved his large hands up her arms to her shoulders. ''Now you just need to relax.''

''I am relaxed,'' she lied.

''You're stiff as a concrete post.'' His fingers worked at the knotted muscles on her shoulders. ''And every time I touch you, a look of sheer terror comes over your face. What are you so afraid of?''

Her knees went weak when his fingertips massaged the nape of her neck. Heat curled from the top of her head and worked its way through her limbs, then pooled low in her belly. ''I'm not afraid,'' she insisted. ''I just don't...think of you that way, that's all.''

He lifted one brow. ''What way?''

''You know.'' Abby felt her cheeks burn. ''*That* way.''

"Oh." His hands were moving on her shoulders again. "So what way *do* you think of me, then?"

His thumbs were moving in slow circles over her collarbone. She resisted the urge to close her eyes and lean into him. "Professionally," she responded.

"Well, there's the problem, then," he said thoughtfully. "We need to change the way you think about me. Just for two weeks, of course."

"But—"

"No buts." He put a finger to her mouth, gently rubbed her bottom lip. "There's that look again, Abby. Ruby and Emerald are going to get suspicious if you panic every time I touch you."

She was too paralyzed to panic. Her heart pounded so furiously she was certain he could hear it. The masculine scent of him, the heat of his skin, the rough texture of his fingertip on her mouth. If he wasn't still holding her with his other hand, she was certain she'd slip to the floor.

She blinked, forced herself to remember she was a grown woman, that he was simply trying to help her out of an embarrassing and difficult situation with her aunts. So maybe she was attracted to him a little. Or maybe even more than a little. Maybe a lot. So what? He certainly wasn't attracted to her, so this had nowhere to go. What harm could it do if she did pretend for a few days? She might actually enjoy it.

"I'm not afraid," she whispered, not sure she could tell the difference between fear and the thrill of his touch. "And I won't panic."

"We need to be sure," he murmured, then slid off her glasses and set them on the desk. "For your aunts' sake."

"Of course." She swallowed the thickness in her throat. "For my aunts' sake."

Callan stared at her mouth, then slowly, so very slowly, lowered his head to hers. She struggled to breathe, told herself it was just a test, an experiment. How else would they know?

The air shimmered with anticipation and still he hadn't actually made contact. A shiver ran through her, her lips parted, waiting…waiting…

Callan hadn't really intended to kiss Abby. He'd just wanted her to relax a little, to be comfortable around him. And what better way to get her to loosen up than to hold her close, to touch her and have her whisper his name? Didn't that always work with other women?

But as he closed the distance between them, as he hovered near enough to feel her soft, sweet breath against his mouth, he wasn't thinking about other women. He wasn't thinking at all.

He had to taste her. Not like that little peck at the restaurant, though that brief brush of lips had intrigued him. No, he needed to really taste her this time. He had to.

He pressed his lips lightly to hers, a whisper of a touch, yet it packed more wallop than a prize-fighter's punch. The shock of pleasure reverberated through him clear down to his boots, then sprang back upward and settled just below his belly. Stunned, he slid his hands down her back, pulling her closer as he eased the kiss deeper. Her lips parted, welcoming, and though he'd certainly never intended tongues to get involved here, his body seemed to suddenly have a mind of its own.

His heart slammed in his chest at the tentative slide of her warm, wet tongue over his. The kiss was as contradictory as the woman herself: wild, yet innocent,

sweet, yet exotic. He'd never experienced anything like
it. Her arms slid around his neck; her breasts pressed
against his chest. Beautiful, soft breasts that he'd
glimpsed briefly just last night and had thought about
much too often. Incredible breasts encased in mint-
green lace. His hands ached to touch them. His mouth
ached to kiss them.

Her low moan brought him back to his senses. This
was Abby, he reminded himself. He couldn't take advantage of her, she didn't know what she was doing.
His body raged at him, but he'd regained just enough
control to win the argument.

Slowly, reluctantly, he broke off the kiss and made
the mistake of looking down at her. Her eyes were
closed, her cheeks flushed, her lips swollen and wet
from his kiss.

Oh, hell.

He was reaching for her again when the outer door
opened and Gabe walked in. His brother froze, stared,
then without a word, turned and walked out again.

Dammit, dammit, dammit.

Wouldn't it just figure? Gabe rarely came to the office, but he just had to pick this exact moment to walk
in. He had no idea how he was going to explain to
Gabe that this was just an experiment, so to speak.
Nothing more than an innocent kiss.

Innocent? He nearly laughed out loud. Who the hell
was he kidding? There'd been nothing innocent about
it at all. That kiss had been downright *hot*.

Which was exactly why he had to put a stop to it
right now.

He took hold of her arms, caught sight of the computer monitor behind them and all he could see was,
"Fatal Error."

That was an understatement.

"Abby."

"Hmm?" She stirred, unintentionally rubbing her breasts against his chest. He clenched his jaw to keep from dragging her into his office and taking her right there on his desk.

"Abby," he said again. "Gabe just walked in."

Her eyes, smoky-green and glazed with desire, opened slowly. "What?"

"My brother just came in, then left again."

"Oh, dear." With a gasp she dropped her arms and jumped away from him. Her face went pale. "Oh, *dear.*"

Not exactly the same words that had come to him, but close enough. "Don't worry about it," he said lightly. "I'll explain it to him later. He'll understand."

The look in her eyes was doubtful. "He will?"

Not in a hundred years. "Of course he will. Gabe can be a little intense, but he's a reasonable man. He knows how important you are to the company. Hell, if I hadn't suggested this, then Gabe would have done it himself."

Though Gabe wasn't the man for the job at all, Callan thought. Gabe would take the whole engagement business much too seriously, and besides, he wasn't even remotely Abby's type. Not that Callan knew what type *was* Abby's, but it certainly wasn't Gabe.

"I'm so sorry." She sank down on her desk chair and closed her eyes. "What a mess I've made of everything."

He wanted to comfort her, reassure her that there was no need to be concerned, but with his body still thrumming from that kiss, he decided it would be better to keep his distance. If he touched her again right now, he might not be so valiant.

Who would have thought that Abigail had that much passion underneath her tailored clothes and rigid manner? Some man was going to be a very lucky guy, Cal decided. He stared at her rosy, still-swollen lips, and his throat went dry. Very lucky.

But all he wanted was a secretary, he told himself. A good secretary was like gold, and Abby was twenty-four karat. He wouldn't risk losing her just because he suddenly seemed to have a raging case of testosterone. He'd been busy these past few months and had seriously neglected a few basic human necessities. Though he hardly thought it prudent to go out on any dates while Emerald and Ruby were around, he would be sure and take care of those needs once they were gone.

"Everything is going to be fine," he said, though he was feeling a little, uh, "tense" at the moment. "And there's nothing to be sorry for, Abby."

"Oh, but there is." She bit her bottom lip, and the tiny, though incredibly sexy, gesture made blood shoot like an arrow to the middle section of Cal's anatomy. She looked at him, her eyes round with misery. "There's something else I haven't told you."

They'd already survived their sudden "engagement" and lunch with her aunts, what else could be so difficult? Cal thought. He'd had no idea that Abby was such a worrier. "Just say it, Abby," he encouraged. "It can't be that bad."

"I—" she hesitated, drew in a deep breath "—I told them that we were living together."

Cal called a family meeting at his apartment late that afternoon. Reese and Gabe were sprawled on the living room sofa, arguing over which game to watch, basket-ball or baseball, while Lucian rooted through the re-frigerator for a beer. Even his sister, Cara, who lived outside of Philadelphia, had made the thirty-minute drive after receiving his cryptic phone call. He hadn't seen much of her since she'd gotten married a few months ago, but he'd been as consumed with his work lately as she'd been with her new husband, Ian, and her new job as vice president of the Killian Shawnessy Foundation that Ian's grandmother had started in her grandson's name.

As the youngest Sinclair, Cara had been teased end-lessly by her four big brothers, but if anyone outside the family said a word, or even looked cross-eyed at their gorgeous blond sister, they'd have had all four Sinclair men to deal with. Her husband, Ian, was her champion now, but Cara would always be his little sis-ter, Cal thought.

She lounged on the ottoman of his ugly brown—though favorite—recliner that belonged in easy chair heaven. His apartment was a decorator's nightmare, a mish-mash of stuff his siblings hadn't wanted. It wasn't that he couldn't afford nicer things. Business was booming, and a few risky ventures in investing had more than paid off. But when he wasn't traveling and looking for new projects to develop, he was busy han-dling the projects that Sinclair Construction was in-volved with in Bloomfield.

He just wasn't around enough right now to take care of a house and yard or spend time worrying if the tile matched the wallpaper or the carpet clashed with the paint. Besides, when he was ready—which wouldn't be for a long time—he'd build his own house, then let the little woman pick all that stuff out. Women were good at that.

He remembered Abby's house. Something like that would be nice. Cozy and warm, with all those flowers and feminine touches. That sofa of hers had been soft and comfortable, but then, he thought, so had Abby. The way she'd curled up in his arms, the feel of her warm, firm breasts pressing against his chest—

"Are we playing Twenty Questions or are you going to tell us why you called us here?" Cara asked, interrupting Callan's train of thought. A train that should have been derailed much sooner, he thought, annoyed with himself that he kept thinking about Abby in a way he didn't want to.

"It better be good." Lucian leaned a shoulder against the kitchen doorjamb. "I left a ten-man crew of framers on the Palmer project by themselves, and I still have to rough in the electrical panel before the inspector comes in the morning. What gives, Cal?"

"He wants to tell us that he's engaged," Reese said bluntly. "To Abigail."

Cal glared at Reese, who'd grabbed the remote away from a slack-jawed Gabe and turned on the baseball game. The bottle of beer that had been halfway to Lucian's mouth froze. Cara stared mutely.

Dammit, anyway, this wasn't exactly how he'd wanted to break the news.

Gabe recovered first. "What the *hell* is he talking about?"

Lucian narrowed his eyes and pushed away from the doorjamb. "You're *what?* To *who?*"

The sound of cheering fans from the television broke the stunned silence. Reese gave a hoot of approval and, eyes glued to the game, settled back on the sofa.

Cara stood, snatched the remote control from Reese's hand and snapped the TV off.

"Hey," Reese protested. "That was the bottom of the ninth, two outs, tied score with two men on base."

"It will give you something to look forward to on the news later." Cara slid an "I'm waiting" look to Cal.

"We're not really engaged, for crying out loud," Cal said irritably. "Abigail and I are just pretending for a few days while her Aunt Emerald and Aunt Ruby are in town."

"Well, that makes sense to me." Lucian took a swig of beer and looked at the rest of his siblings. "How 'bout you guys?"

"Oh, sure." Gabe's look was bland. "Perfect sense."

"Absolutely." Cara pressed her lips together.

Exasperated, Cal jammed his hands on his hips and frowned at Gabe and Lucian. "Look, I wasn't about to let the best secretary we ever had quit."

Lucian's brows drew together. "Abigail was going to quit?"

Gabe shook his head. "Abigail wouldn't quit."

"Well, she did quit," Callan said. "She was gone when I got back from Woodbury yesterday. If you guys showed up at the office once in a while, you'd have known."

"You're in charge of the office and site production," Lucian argued. "Abigail's your responsibility."

"One he takes quite seriously, based on the lip lock he gave her this afternoon in the office," Gabe said dryly.

Lucian choked on the beer he'd just swallowed. Cara

narrowed her eyes. Reese, who'd been sitting back enjoying the show, suddenly leaned forward, eyes wide.

"You kissed Abigail?" Lucian finally managed. "Our Abigail?"

"How was it?" Reese piped up, then grimaced when Cara smacked his head with her hand.

Cal sucked in a breath through his clenched teeth. So much for family support. "It wasn't like that. I just wanted her to relax a little, so her aunts wouldn't be suspicious."

"For God's sake, Cal," Gabe groaned. "What the hell are you talking about?"

"It's kind of a funny story." He gave a dry laugh, but no one joined him. "You see, Abby's aunts, Ruby and Emerald, felt that she should have a man in her life to, well, take care of her, I guess. So after Abby moved to Bloomfield, she told her aunts that she had a man, not only to ease their minds, but so they'd finally go on the cruise they'd always wanted to go on, but wouldn't take until Abby was settled."

"And this has what to do with you and Sinclair Construction?" Gabe asked.

"Well—" Callan stuck his hands into the back pockets of his jeans "—she told them that I was the man in her life, that we'd gotten engaged."

"To *you?*" Lucian laughed. "Why would she pick *you?*"

Cal narrowed his eyes. "Why wouldn't she pick me?"

"Well, everyone knows I'm the best-looking Sinclair." Lucian winked at his sister. "Except for Cara, of course, but she's a girl."

"Who says you're the best looking?" Reese argued.

"Besides Irma Johnson, who's seventy-four and blind as a bat."

"Knock it off." Scowling, Gabe stood. As the oldest, he had the most clout and respect in the Sinclair family. Even Lucian, who had the hottest temper, conceded to Gabe. "You're telling us that you and Abigail are pretending to be engaged so her aunts will leave her alone and go on a trip?"

"Why not? Abby will be happy, her aunts will be happy, and I will keep the best secretary we could ever hope to have. Simple as that."

"And what happens down the road, when you don't get married?" Cara asked. "Then what?"

Hell, he didn't know. That was down the road. One problem at a time. "We'll figure that out then," he said defensively. "Or maybe we'll tell them we broke it off and she's seeing someone else. Who knows, maybe she'll have a real fiancé by then."

Cara shook her head. "You're playing with fire here, Cal. Someone's going to get hurt."

He thought of the kiss they'd shared earlier and felt his skin heat up. Just a fluke, he told himself. If he kissed her again, which he wasn't going to, he was certain his reaction would be more…controlled.

"No one's going to get hurt," he insisted. "And I'm not playing with fire, I'm putting one out. So if Abby and I have to do a little hand holding and live together for a few days, then fine."

"Live together?"

They all said it at the same time, which was exactly the reaction he'd been expecting. Which was also why he'd left that little piece of information until last.

"We're rational adults with no involvement beyond work." Even Abby herself had told him that she didn't think of him *that* way, hadn't she? And he didn't think of her *that* way, either. At least nothing he couldn't keep under control.

"I'll sleep in the spare bedroom, drop a few guy things around to make it look good. Once Emerald and Ruby are gone, everything will go back to the way it was."

"You really believe that?" Cara arched one delicate brow. She had that woman-look in her eyes, one that said, "You men can be so stupid."

"Of course I believe it." A tingling sensation scurried up Cal's neck, and he rubbed at it. "Completely."

He did believe it.

Absolutely.

Without a doubt.

In two weeks, he told himself, they'd all have a good laugh about it, and life would be back to normal. No more pretending to be engaged and in love, and certainly no living together.

A sweet, simple plan, if he did say so, and gave himself a mental pat on the back.

Five

Abby had a routine: she showered at precisely 6:30 a.m. every morning, after first picking up her paper and making coffee. She dressed, left her house at 7:45 and arrived at the office at 7:55. She turned her computer on and was ready for work at 8:00.

Her life was structured, predictable. Exactly the way she wanted it.

This morning, however, she'd stepped into the shower at 6 a.m. Not only because she'd been awake, anyway, but because she was certain that would give her plenty of time to be in and out of the bathroom and dressed before Callan woke up.

Despite her protests and insistence that she tell her aunts the truth, he'd shown up at her door last night, canvas sports bag in hand, and settled into her spare bedroom.

She'd slept very little last night.

Abby had never lived with a man before. Not that she was exactly living with one now, she reminded herself abruptly as she reached for her shampoo. But to see a baseball cap hanging casually from a coat hook in her entry, a black leather wallet and car keys on the top of her kitchen bar and shaving cream on her bathroom counter, well, it almost felt as if Callan *were* actually living at her house.

Lathering a generous portion of shampoo into her thick hair, she thought about him sleeping in her house, in her guest bed. All night. With only one wall separating them. Her pulse started to race.

Imagine. Callan Sinclair. Living in Abigail Thomas's house.

She smiled.

Her smiled faded as she caught the scent of something woodsy. Frowning, she looked at the shampoo bottle she'd set back on her shower shelf and realized it wasn't hers. It was Callan's.

Wide-eyed, she stared at the black plastic bottle. He must have put it in her shower last night when he'd unpacked his things. She realized that she'd just washed her hair with *his* shampoo.

It felt so…personal. So *intimate*.

A shiver wiggled up her spine.

Breathing in the masculine scent, she tipped her head back and rinsed the lather from her head, felt the thick suds slide down her back, her thighs, her legs. Her breasts felt tight and tingly. She remembered the feel of his chest underneath her when she'd woken up with him on the sofa, the way he'd kissed her in the office yesterday and made her bones feel soft. She'd thought about that kiss all day and night, the press of his lips on hers, the sweep of his tongue.

She'd been kissed before. She certainly wasn't completely ignorant of men. When she'd been living in New York with her aunts, she'd dated more men than she'd ever wanted to, though none seriously. She'd always thought that kissing was pleasant, but *pleasant* didn't come close to what she'd felt with Callan. *Destroyed* was fairly accurate. Utterly and completely devastated.

But it meant nothing to him. Not living in her house, not waking up with her half-naked on top of him, not even the kiss he'd given her. As he'd told her, he'd only been trying to make her relax. Even though he'd seemed to enjoy it, too, she couldn't let herself think, even for a moment, that it actually meant anything to him beyond the role he was playing.

What had he said to Ray Palmer? "Abigail's a valuable asset to Sinclair Construction, and we would never let her go."

And if that meant kissing plain little Abby, then that's what he'd do.

Shutting off the shower, she dried herself quickly with a thick blue towel, pulled on a pink floral robe and dragged a comb through her wavy hair. She reached for her face moisturizer, then hesitated when she saw Callan's can of shaving lotion on the counter.

She glanced at the closed door, then back at the shaving cream. She couldn't help herself. She had to smell it.

She popped off the cap and sniffed the nozzle. Though it was a different smell than the shampoo, it had a woodsy aroma, too. She breathed in the masculine scent, felt a fluttering in her stomach. Unable to stop herself, she squeezed a puff of foam onto her fingertips. The consistency was thicker than what she used on her legs, more firm. She stared in the mirror and swiped the cream across her jaw, amazed at how smooth and slick it felt on her skin.

"Abby? You almost done in there?"

With a gasp she dropped the can in the sink. It landed with a loud, metallic crash.

"You okay?" Callan asked.

"Just a minute," she squeaked.

Oh, dear, oh, dear. Abby scooped up the can, clicked the top back on and set it on the countertop, hoping she put it in the same place as it was before. Heart pounding, she snatched a towel from its hook and quickly wiped the cream off her face.

She dragged in three deep breaths, tightened the sash on her robe and opened the door.

And then she couldn't breathe at all.

Bare-chested, he stood there, arms on both sides of the door. Dark, rumpled hair and a morning beard, he was every woman's fantasy. Her knees felt weak as she stared at him.

"You all right?"

His voice, gravelly and deep, skimmed over her still-damp skin like a hand.

"Of course." Her voice cracked. "I wasn't expecting you up so soon."

He yawned, a big, manly yawn that fascinated her. "Me, neither. A blue jay was tapping at the window and woke me up. Friend of yours?"

Oh, dear. With all the confusion in her life, she'd forgotten about the bird. "That's Stanley. He goes around the house and taps on the windows when I forget to put peanuts out for his breakfast. I'm sorry."

"Stanley?" Callan chuckled and shook his head. "Abby, you are a remarkable woman."

His compliment warmed her, as did his closeness. Standing there, early in the morning, at the bathroom door, anyone just might believe that they were a couple.

But they weren't. Maybe friends, she decided, though even friends might be too awkward if they were going to continue to work together. Callan Sinclair was her boss. Her employer. That was all.

She straightened her shoulders. "I'm finished in here. You can have the bathroom now."

She stepped toward him, expecting him to move out of the way. He didn't. He just stared at her.

"How come you don't wear your hair like that?" he asked softly.

Startled by his question, she touched the ends of her shoulder-length hair. "Wet?"

He smiled. "No, although that looks nice, too. I mean down. You have pretty hair."

She swallowed hard. "Thank you."

Her heart jumped when he reached out and touched her face. He dragged one rough finger across the underside of her jaw, then he pulled it away and raised his brows. "Abby, do you shave your face?"

Oh, no, no, no.

"Certainly not," she choked out. "I…I must have had some shaving cream on my hand—after I shaved my legs, I mean."

He rubbed the cream in his fingers and smiled. "I was kidding, Abby. You've really got to learn to loosen up."

He stepped out of the way then, and she brushed past.

"Mind if I have some of that coffee you made?" he called as she hurried down the hall to her bedroom.

"Help yourself to anything you like," she said, and when the thought, *including me,* popped into her mind, she nearly gasped out loud.

Inside her bedroom, she closed the door and sank down on the edge of her bed. Two weeks, she told herself. Then her aunts would be gone, and she and Callan could put an end to this ridiculous charade. She could certainly hang in there for two weeks, for Heaven's sake.

She pressed her fingertips to her jaw; her skin still felt warm from Callan's touch.

And two weeks suddenly felt like a lifetime.

"I finished the breakdowns and bonding information on the Gibson project, mailed out the subdivision report on the Walker job and made triple copies of the insurance certificates for Mr. Palmer. I sent a fax to Lucian at the site trailer, but I do think you should look at the upgrades Mr. Palmer's requested. They aren't as substantial as the last ones, but I believe you should at least be aware of the changes…"

Callan sat at his desk and stared at the open file Abby had laid on his desk, half listening as she methodically went over the report she'd worked up. Dressed in her usual, stiff business suit, her hair pulled tightly back and her glasses perched on her nose, she stood opposite him, reading from the copy in her hands.

He'd been living in her house for the past week, working with her, and though he would have expected to be going stir-crazy, spending so much time with one woman, he found he hadn't minded at all.

Not that he was getting soft on settling down, or anything as drastic as that, he just thought that maybe he could understand why, when the right woman came along, some guys went for that sort of thing. Home-cooked meals sure beat out a frozen dinner any night, it was nice saying good-morning and good-night to someone, and sharing a bed with someone you cared about certainly had its advantages.

Not that he thought about Abby that way, Callan quickly reminded himself. Well, he supposed he did *think* about the sharing-a-bed part, but he had no intention of doing anything more than think. She was his secretary, and that's the way he wanted to keep it.

He realized he'd taken her for granted before, but that was all in the past now. He was a new man. A more sensitive, thoughtful kind of guy. That's what women wanted, didn't they? Understanding, patience, compassion. How hard could that be?

From now on, if Abby had a problem, she'd know she could come to him. She didn't have to quit or run away. Together they'd find a solution.

Of course, pretending to be engaged and sleeping at her house was a bit extreme, he realized, but desperate times called for desperate measures. If it meant her staying with Sinclair Construction, then sleeping in her guest bed and sharing a bathroom for the past four days had been small concessions, Callan thought. Not to mention interesting ones.

Especially that first morning, when he'd seen her come out of the bathroom wearing that pretty floral robe. With her wet hair brushing her shoulders, her skin flushed and the steam swirling around her, she'd made quite an enticing sight.

Damn if he hadn't been tempted to taste those lips of hers again, right there in the bathroom, but after that kiss in the office the other day, he wasn't taking any chances. If he stepped over any boundaries, he might lose Abby, and he couldn't, wouldn't, let that happen. She was much too important to him to throw away on any impulsive…urges.

He just had to stop thinking of her as a woman, that's all. He could do that for the sake of his business.

During working hours he had been careful to keep his distance from her, intentionally staying at the job sites longer than necessary, but he'd had to come back to her place in the evenings. To keep up appearances, of course, since Emerald and Ruby had been over to Abby's every evening to visit. He didn't want them to wonder why he was never there, then get suspicious, but because he was afraid he might somehow trip up and expose the "plot," he'd stayed out of their way as best he could and avoided any in-depth discussions with them.

And it seemed to him, especially when Emerald and Ruby weren't around, that Abby had been avoiding him, as well.

Yet in spite of the fact that she went straight to her bedroom after her aunts left and got up earlier than Stanley the blue jay, whom she fed peanuts to every morning, Callan had still managed to learn a few things about Abigail Thomas.

She grew her own tomatoes and squash, was an amazing cook and, except for reading, she didn't need those glasses she wore all day at work. She also liked to go barefoot in the house, though she wore slacks or long skirts and kept her legs covered. It surprised him that she painted her toenails deep red, and more than once in the past week he'd caught himself staring at her feet.

He glanced down, thought about those pretty red toe-nails and smooth feet underneath those ugly shoes, and

God help him, he couldn't stop himself from wondering what she was wearing under that shapeless tan suit she had on....

He jerked himself out of his thoughts, forced himself to concentrate on her voice, then wondered why he'd never noticed before how smooth it was, how soft.

"...a minor architectural adjustment on the façade in the main entrance," she was saying. "Instead of flat, straight columns, he's decided that archways and curves will add more interest..."

Curves definitely add more interest, Callan agreed, and his gaze wandered over Abby. Was she wearing that sexy, green lace bra she had on the other night? And though he hadn't seen them, he'd bet a week's draw she had matching panties.

"If you'd like, I can order several in different colors for you to look at," Abigail said.

He blinked, then glanced up sharply. "What?"

She tilted her head down and looked at him over her glasses. "The new tile Mr. Palmer requested. For the fountain in the courtyard."

Dammit, he had to keep his mind on the job, not on Abby's underwear. "Right. Go ahead and order several. In different colors. Whatever you like."

She looked at him curiously. "Whatever I like?"

"That's right. You choose."

"All right." She cleared her throat. "I'll have them delivered to Mr. Palmer before his inspection next week."

"That's a good—" He paused, then frowned. "Inspection?"

"You're picking Mr. Palmer and his son, Jack, up from the airport next Tuesday at two in the afternoon, then driving them out to the job site for an inspection.

I've made six-o'clock dinner reservations for three at Sanderson's Steak House and booked a suite at the Colonial West Inn.''

Frowning, she stepped beside him and glanced over his shoulder at his desk appointment calendar. ''Didn't I write it down?''

Callan frowned. He'd been so distracted the past few days with Abby and her aunts, he'd nearly forgotten about Palmer's visit. Ray canceled or rescheduled his inspections with the same regularity he changed his architectural plans, and already the project was two months behind schedule. Callan hadn't met Ray's son yet, but he could imagine that Jack Palmer was just as big a pain in the butt as his father. And if he looked anything like his father, he was five-four and bald. Callan looked forward to spending an entire afternoon and evening with the two men as much as he would a blister on his foot.

But Ray Palmer was not only one of the wealthiest developers out of Boston, he was also Sinclair Construction's biggest client. So if the man wanted to go to dinner, then fine, dinner it was.

''Here it is.'' Abby leaned over him and pointed to his desk calendar. ''Two o'clock. Airport. Ray and Jack Palmer. Dinner at six.''

He caught the scent of her as she leaned over him and brushed against his arm. Something feminine and lightly floral. It seeped into his senses and played havoc there. Made him wonder if she smelled like that all over.

If she were any other woman, he'd find out. He'd slip off that stiff jacket of hers, then unbutton her prim white blouse and lay her back on his desk and—

He caught himself before his fantasy went any further. Once again he reminded himself that Abby wasn't any other woman. She was *Abby*.

With a sigh he leaned back in his chair, then glanced at his watch. It was 5:45. "Aren't we supposed to meet Emerald and Ruby for dinner at the tavern about now?"

Abby nodded apologetically. "If you'd rather not go, I can tell them you have to work late. They'd understand."

"And miss the fabulous Bliss Sisters in concert?" He stood and was already leading her out of his office. "Reese said that yesterday their rendition of "Hello Dolly" made the lunch crowd go wild."

Abby closed her eyes on a shudder. "How 'bout you go without me and tell them that I had to work?"

"Abby." He took her by her arms and turned her to face him. "Your aunts are terrific. A little impulsive maybe, a little outrageous. But what's the harm in that?"

She stared at him for a long time, and there was something in her eyes he couldn't read. Sadness, maybe? Longing?

"No harm," she said softly, then pulled away from him and reached for her purse. "Shall we go?"

Because she'd loaned her car to her aunts for the week, Callan had been driving Abby to and from work every day. Strange, but he'd enjoyed the few minutes they spent alone on the ride, not talking, just listening to the radio. It felt…comfortable. He couldn't remember ever feeling that way around any other woman before.

When they reached the tavern, he parked, then came around and opened the truck door for Abby. Her hand felt small and warm in his, and he resisted the temptation to pull her against him as she slid out of the truck. He stared at her soft, lush mouth, felt a bolt of desire shoot through him.

You're playing with fire. His sister's words came back to him. *Someone's going to get hurt.*

He blinked, dropped the hand that had already been reaching for Abby. It *was* playing with fire, and dammit, he wasn't going to hurt Abby. She was special to him, and she deserved better than a lustful, quick roll in the hay.

It was just all this pretend business that was getting to him, he told himself, like the touching and the occasional quick kisses they'd shared over the week when Emerald and Ruby were around. Once her aunts were gone, Callan was certain the fantasies he kept having about him and Abby would stop.

He sucked in a deep breath and gestured toward the tavern. "After you," he said, forcing a light tone.

The sound of music poured from the tavern into the cool night air, as did the din of the crowd inside. Callan opened the door for Abby, and when she stepped inside, the place went strangely quiet.

"Surprise!"

Six

Abby's eyes went wide at the sight of the crowded tavern. Every person in the place stared at her and Callan. Emerald and Ruby, dressed in brightly colored sequins and beads and grinning ear to ear, stood under a handmade paper banner strung over the bar that read Congratulations Abby and Callan.

Oh, dear. Oh dear, dear, *dear!*

It seemed as though the entire town was packed into the room, and all at once they moved forward, shouting best wishes and congratulations. The men slapped Callan's back and shook his hand, while the women hugged and kissed her.

"We're so happy for you."

"You make such a darling couple."

"Who would have ever guessed?"

This couldn't be happening, Abby thought as she

was passed from one embrace to the next. It couldn't be.

Ruby and Emerald.

Her aunts had arranged all this. She should have known, should have suspected what they were up to, but she'd been so distracted with Callan staying in her house all week that she'd let her guard down.

She'd made a terrible mistake not keeping a closer eye on her aunts, and now Callan was going to be furious with her. He would probably never speak to her again, she thought wildly.

She tried to find him over the sea of heads, but suddenly found herself swept up in a strong pair of arms.

"Welcome to the family, Sis," Gabe Sinclair said with a grin, then kissed her soundly on the mouth.

Good Heavens! Eyes wide, she stared at him, though with his mouth plastered to hers, she couldn't speak. Gabe, the most serious Sinclair brother, was actually *kissing* her.

Before she could draw in a breath, her glasses were snatched off her nose, and she felt herself wrenched from Gabe's hold, then pulled into another pair of equally strong and equally muscular arms.

"My turn, Bro."

This time it was Lucian kissing her. *Lucian,* of all people! Lucian, with the short fuse and long temper, had his mouth sealed over hers like a stamp on an envelope.

She heard the cheers and shouts all around her, but her head was spinning so fast, that if Lucian hadn't been holding her, she would have crumpled to the floor.

And then she was dragged from Lucian's arms into Reese's, and she couldn't think at all. Reese Sinclair, obviously determined to outdo his brothers on time and intensity, fused his mouth to hers. She felt the laughter roll in Reese's chest as the men surrounding them hooted and hollered, felt her face burn with embarrassment at the enthusiasm with which he applied himself to the kiss.

She'd had no idea that the Sinclair men were so arduous, so passionate. So idiotic.

"That's enough, little brother," Abby heard a wonderfully familiar voice growl beside her.

This time when she was yanked from Reese, she found herself in the final Sinclair brother's arms. Callan, his face a tight mask, pulled her close to him, effectively cutting off any more amorous attempts from his brothers or anyone else in the crowd. She sank against him, nearly cried at the wonderful feel of his strong arms around her. She knew he was angry, but she clung to him, anyway, desperate to pull herself together before she had to face anyone else.

Callan leaned his head down and whispered in her ear, "You okay?"

She nodded, drew in a long, deep, fortifying breath and held it in her lungs.

Aunt Ruby started to clang on a bell hanging on the wall beside the bar. "Attention, everyone. May I have your attention."

When the crowd quieted, Abby thought for certain they could all hear the wild pounding of her heart. As much as she loved her aunts, at the moment Abby could have strangled them both.

"As you all know," Emerald said loudly, "this is an engagement party for our beautiful niece, Abigail Thomas, and her handsome fiancé, Callan Sinclair."

As the crowd erupted into whistles and cheers, someone thrust a glass of champagne into Abby's shaking hand. Emerald waited until she had everyone's attention, then paused with all the dramatic skill of a lifetime onstage.

"To our darling Abby." Emerald raised her glass of champagne. "'May you always be happy, and live at your ease, get a kind husband and do as you please.'"

The women cheered at Emerald's toast, and when Ruby stepped forward and held up her glass, the room quieted again. "To Callan, 'May your love for Abby be great and true, and tell me, dear, are there any others at home like you?'"

Ruby nearly brought the roof down with her outrageous toast. The men slapped the other three Sinclair men on the backs while the women shrieked. Even Callan laughed at all the nonsense, and when Abby glanced up at him, it almost appeared as though he really *was* having a good time. How could he? she wondered. In the midst of all this chaos, this charade, this *humiliation*, how could he possibly be having fun?

Her own smile was forced, maybe he was simply putting on a front, too. After all, what else was there to do? They couldn't very well stand up and say, "Gee, thanks, anyway, but we aren't really engaged, we were just pretending for Abby's aunts."

She downed the glass of champagne, tried not to wince at the unpleasant taste, then nodded at all the people who were wishing them well. Some were complete strangers, but others—Mr. Weldon from the drugstore, Jane Needham, the manager at the market, Richard from the post office—these were people she knew and saw regularly. How was she ever going to face them again?

And Callan's sister, Cara. Abby spotted her sitting at the bar with her husband, Ian, watching, an amused but wary smile on her face. She must know the truth, Abby thought. Callan must have told her, just as he must have told his brothers. But here they were, all celebrating and having a good time as if this truly were an engagement.

Crazy. This whole thing was insane. And it was her own fault, she thought miserably. She'd brought this entire nightmare on herself.

All because of one teensy-weensy lie to her aunts. Abby swore to herself that once this was through, she was never, ever, going to tell even the tiniest lie again.

"Speech! Speech!"

Abby's heart sank at the crowd's demand. Both she and Callan were pushed and prodded to a small, raised stage at the back of the bar. Maybe Callan would decide he'd had enough of all this and simply tell the truth, Abby thought. Right here in front of the entire town he would admit that he'd only been trying to help poor little Abigail Thomas out of a tight spot.

When they reached center stage, Callan draped a possessive arm around her shoulder and pulled her close as he looked out at everyone. The room quieted once again, with only a few heckles from the men about matrimony. Breath held, Abby stared over all the heads. Her hands felt icy and stiff.

"Some of you might be surprised that Abby and I are engaged," Callan began, "but I think it would be fair to say that no one is more surprised than we are. It's truly a mystery how things like this happen." He squeezed her shoulder. "We were going to keep it just between us for a while, but since you all know about it now, well—" he lowered his voice "—we'd like to ask you not to tell anyone else."

The room burst into laughter at Callan's request.

Since it seemed as though a great portion of the town seemed to be in the room, he was obviously making a joke. When he grinned down at her and winked, she could only stare at him in disbelief. Here they were, on display, caught in a bald-faced lie, and he was making fun!

"Give her a kiss, Sinclair," someone shouted, and everyone joined in until it became a chant. Emerald and Ruby stood in front of the crowd, their eyes brimming with tears.

Panic filled Abby. Even if she'd wanted to run, she couldn't have, her knees were shaking so badly. It was one thing for him to kiss her in front of her aunts for show, or that one time in the office when no one else was around. But here, in front of all these people!

She felt her pulse hammering in her temple, couldn't seem to bring air into her lungs, but when Callan lowered his face and pressed his lips to hers, they could have been on the Superbowl field with the stands filled and it wouldn't have mattered.

Her mind simply went blank.

She did hear the shouting and encouragement, but it sounded as if it were far away, muffled, as if she had cotton in her ears. He pulled her closer, and she leaned into him, parting her lips as he deepened the kiss. Her blood pounded through her veins, her nerves felt raw and exposed. She felt the crackle of electricity jumping over her skin, heard the soft moan rise from deep in her throat.

If she wasn't still holding on to the thinnest thread of control, she would have dragged him closer, deepened the kiss even more, slid her hands over his broad chest and steel-like muscles. Instead, she held her palms flat on his chest, felt the warmth of his skin through his shirt even as she felt the heavy thud of his heartbeat.

With a gasp, Abby broke off the kiss, shocked by her public response to Callan's kiss. She stared into his eyes, saw the surprise there, as well. And something else. Something dark and sensuous and very primitive. She shivered from the force of it, then felt the heat of her blush on her cheeks.

Everyone in the room cheered loudly, and when a slow, sexy song filled the tavern, they shouted for the happy couple to dance.

Dear Lord, Abby thought, but this was going to be a long night.

Because he was still on fire from the kiss he and Abby had just shared, Callan welcomed the opportunity to simply dance with her and ignore everyone in the room. He needed a minute before he could gather his wits about him again, and several more before his body returned to a more ''comfortable'' state. Damn if that kiss hadn't turned him on—and in front of practically the whole blasted town. If she hadn't pulled away when she had, God knew what he might have done.

''Callan, I didn't know about this,'' she whispered. ''I swear I didn't.''

Her warm breath against his ear stirred up flames he'd just barely managed to get under control. To keep his mind off those flames, Callan concentrated on his dancing and managed a fancy step that Cara had taught him a few months ago. It surprised him when Abby followed the step without missing a beat.

He shrugged. ''It was bound to come out sooner or later, especially in this town. At least now we don't have to worry about who knows and who doesn't.''

"Because everyone knows," she said, closing her eyes. "I'm so sorry."

He smiled at another couple dancing by, then smoothly turned her. Once again she followed him as if they'd been dancing together for years. "Abby, there's nothing to be sorry about. We wanted to convince your aunts we were engaged, didn't we? After that kiss, I'd say we were pretty damn convincing, wouldn't you? Hell," he said with a dry laugh, "if I didn't know better, even I'd have thought that was the real thing."

He glanced down at her, wanting to see her face. He wasn't sure why he felt disappointed that she was looking the other way and he couldn't read her eyes.

"I've caused you so much trouble," she said quietly.

"Stop worrying," he told her, strangely annoyed she'd said nothing about the kiss. "Just relax and enjoy the party."

"You don't understand." She shook her head. "When it comes to Emerald and Ruby, you can't relax. It's much too dangerous."

He laughed at her then, and for appearances only, he told himself, hugged her to him, thinking how good she felt in his arms. It amazed him how well her body fit against his. How well they moved together. He attempted a complicated step, certain that she'd stumble and he could pull her up closer to him, but she followed him without blinking an eye. In fact, she hadn't even seemed to notice.

Damn, he'd always impressed the ladies he'd danced with before. Frowning, he searched his brain for any other steps that Cara had shown him, but he'd pretty much used up his moves.

When Abby suddenly stiffened in his arms and drew

in a sharp breath, he looked down at her. Her eyes were wide, her lips parted in horror.

"What?" He glanced in the direction she was staring. A man dressed in a tight black T-shirt and pants, his black hair slicked back in a fifties-style pompadour, was smiling at Abby.

"Roberto," she gasped.

"Who the hell is Roberto?" Callan narrowed his eyes as he glared at the man. He reminded Callan of someone, but he wasn't sure who.

Abby was already turning in the opposite direction to the man, making her way through the other couples dancing. "I knew they'd do something like this. I have to go."

"Do something like what?" He followed after her, but not before giving Roberto another fierce look. "Who the hell is that guy?"

"I can't explain now. I'm sorry, but—"

"Abby!" Ruby stepped in front of her niece. "There you are. We have a surprise for you. Roberto's here."

"No, Aunt Ruby, please," Abby pleaded. "Please don't do this."

"Abby, for Heaven's sake, what's wrong with you? The Thomas-Bliss family always performs at celebrations, and the guest of honor is always the star. You know that. Come along, dear."

"I can't. Really, I can't," Abby said frantically. "It's been too long. I…I can't remember."

"Nonsense." Ruby waved a hand at her. "It's like riding a bicycle. You'll be fine. Now come and change."

Callan watched as Abby glanced back at him, her eyes beseeching. He wanted to save her, he just didn't know from what, so he simply waved as Ruby whisked Abby into a back office.

Maybe her aunts wanted her to sing, Callan thought. That would fit in with the family profile. And though Ruby and Emerald could certainly sing, maybe Abby hadn't been blessed with that ability and that's why she was so embarrassed.

A little entertainment could be fun, he thought with a smile. So what if Abby wasn't any good at it? It was just the thing that she needed to loosen up a little.

His smile faded as he glanced back at Roberto. So who the hell was he? Someone she sang with? Callan didn't like it, but he could live with her belting out a couple of songs with this fifties reject, he supposed— then tried not to think about her doing anything else with the guy.

He grabbed a beer from a passing waitress and a little meatball thing on a cracker. Hell, even if he wasn't getting married, that was no reason not to enjoy a good party. And he couldn't wait to hear Abby sing. For her own sake, he just hoped she wasn't *too* bad.

"Lose your fiancée already?"

He glanced down at his sister and took a swig of beer. "Why the hell didn't you tell me about this?"

"And spoil all the fun? Now why would I do that?" She smiled at him, one of those sweet smiles that didn't affect brothers, but made most men go moon-eyed. Like her husband, Ian, who was currently having an intense discussion with Gabe at the bar. Cara and Ian had only been married six months, but Ian was as moon-eyed now as he had been before the wedding. From what Callan had heard, Ian had fought the valiant battle, but finally bit it big-time.

The Sinclair men were made of tougher stuff, Callan thought, and took another smug pull off his beer.

Cara slipped an arm through his and rested her head on his shoulder. "If I didn't know better, Cal, I'd say you have a thing for Abby. Unless you always kiss your secretary until smoke comes out your ears."

He frowned at her. "That was just for show, Sis. Abby is my secretary, that's all. Besides, she's told me that she doesn't think of me that way."

Cara raised her brows. "What way?"

"You know," he said irritably. "*That* way. She just sees me as her boss. 'Professionally' was how she put it."

"Oh." Cara's eyes were bright with amusement. "So the way she looks at you, the way she kissed you, that was strictly 'professional.'"

"That's right." He started to take another swig of beer and stopped the bottle halfway. "What way does she look at me?"

"As if she wants to cover you in whipped cream and gobble you up," Cara said with a grin. "In one bite."

The image made his heart stop, then jump. "Don't be ridiculous. We work well together, that's all."

"You dance well together, too. At least, she does," Cara teased.

"Don't you have to take food or drink to your husband, like a good little wife?" Callan asked. His sister's comments were starting to get on his nerves.

And so was waiting for Abby. What was taking so long?

The lights flashed then, and Emerald took center stage. Roberto lurked in the background, and Callan frowned darkly at him.

"Sing us a song, Emmy," Charles Waters, the manager at Mackintosh Department Store, yelled out.

"Maybe later, Charlie," Emmy replied sweetly, "but for now the spotlight is on Callan and Abby. Abby's getting ready, so we'll start with Callan."

Start with Callan? The beer that had been halfway to his mouth froze in midair. His throat went dry. He never agreed to starting anything.

His brothers suddenly had him surrounded and were pushing him toward the stage while the crowd shouted encouragement. Emerald slipped an arm through his and pulled him the rest of the way. Dammit, dammit, *dammit.*

"Since we really didn't know what Callan could do," Emerald said to the crowd, "Ruby and I asked his brothers to choose a song that they know he likes."

When a microphone was shoved in his hand and a pair of sunglasses slipped on his face, Callan decided that he would kill all three of his brothers. Slowly and painfully.

When the music started, Bob Seger's "Old-Time Rock and Roll," he scowled at all of his siblings and brother-in-law, who had lined up in the front row to watch. They were obviously having a good time at his expense.

Oh, what the hell. Callan sighed. Poor Abby was going to have to endure the same indignity, so why not be a good sport? He lifted the microphone…

He missed a few words and more than a few notes, but the crowd cheered him on. His brothers and brother-in-law laughed at him, while Cara just shook her head and rolled her eyes, but Callan had to admit he'd done a decent job by the time he'd finished.

Emerald praised his efforts as she took the microphone back and shooed him off the stage. New music started up again, familiar, but Callan couldn't place it yet. The lights on the stage went dark.

"And now, ladies and gentlemen—" Emerald moved to the side of the stage "—from her starring role in the hit musical *Grease,* we present to you Abigail Thomas, playing Sandy, and Roberto Santini, playing Danny Zuko."

The music grew louder, and Callan recognized it now as the final number between Olivia Newton-John and John Travolta in the movie. *That's* who Roberto looked like, Callan realized. John Travolta twenty years ago.

And Abby played the starring role? *His* Abby? Stunned, he watched in amazement as the lights flipped back on and lit a woman from behind, leaving only a silhouette.

His mouth dropped open.

Dressed in skin-tight black pants, black leather jacket and spiked high heels, she was all curves. One never-ending leg was bent, her toe pointed, and she held her head to the side, frozen in place while the music continued to pound.

Roberto stood opposite her, clasped his hand to his heart and began to sing that he had chills.

That's when she started to move. First the hips, then the shoulders as she turned toward Roberto and pointed a finger. Her hair was…big…her lips bright-red and eyes smoky.

Abby? This couldn't be Abby.

Abby was shy…and sweet…and…plain.

This woman was devastating. Completely and absolutely.

When she ripped off her leather jacket and tossed it

behind her, any blood that Callan might have had in his brain went south. Her low-cut, off-the-shoulder black spandex top left little to the imagination and much to fantasy. She started to sing, loud and clear and strong, something about needing a man. Roberto followed her around the stage, then fell to his knees at her feet as she told him that he needed to shape up, and she needed a man to keep her satisfied.

Every man in the place was whistling and hollering, including his brothers, whom he would have throttled if he could have taken his eyes off Abby. When she ran her hands sensuously down her body and told Roberto to "feel his way," Callan gripped the beer bottle in his hand so tightly he thought it might break.

The number continued, rose to a fever pitch when Roberto picked her up, and she wrapped her legs around him as they finished the song.

Callan wanted to kill the guy.

When Abby and Roberto took their bows, the crowd went wild, screaming and yelling for more. Abby smiled and waved as naturally as if she did this every night. When her eyes finally met his, her smile slowly faded. She backed away, then turned and ran off the stage.

His jaw set tight, he followed.

Seven

Abby stepped out of the tavern's back exit into the alley. Her legs were shaking so badly she had to lean against the brick wall to hold herself upright. The sound of rustling in the trash cans made her jump, and when a small mouse darted across the alley, she closed her eyes and sagged back against the wall.

How appropriate, she thought with a shiver. Abigail Thomas—afraid of a mouse.

But not nearly as afraid as she was of having to face Callan again. After the exhibition she'd just put on, how could she ever look at him again, let alone work with him? She'd seen the shock on his face, the confusion, as he'd stared at her on the stage.

Even with the cool night air on her skin, she could feel her face burn. Of all the numbers for her aunts to have chosen for her, why the one with the least amount of clothing and the most bumps and grinds? She

thought of what she must have looked like, with these
skintight clothes and all that wiggling the dance called
for. And in front of nearly the entire town!

Well, she wasn't going back inside, and since she
didn't have her own car, she would just have to walk
home. She glanced down at the four-inch heels on her
feet and sighed. Even though she didn't live far, it was
still going to be a long walk.

The sound of Emerald and Ruby singing drifted from
inside the tavern, and Abby knew that her aunts
wouldn't notice her missing for a little while. She'd
have time to walk home and call the tavern to leave a
message for them that she hadn't been feeling well.

And as for Callan, she thought, pushing away from
the wall and picking her way out of the alley to the
sidewalk, well, she would certainly understand if he'd
had enough of her family's nonsense. She'd heard her
aunts force him to sing on stage, and from what little
she'd heard while getting dressed for her number, she
hadn't thought him half-bad.

Still, he was probably furious about being shoved
into the spotlight the way he was. After her performance Abby had seen the tight set of his jaw as he'd
stared at her.

She passed by Wagner's Veterinarian Clinic, then
the hair salon, rubbing at the goose bumps on her arms.
Her feet were already starting to hurt, but she only had
two more blocks to go. As soon as she got home—
right after she scrubbed her face, combed out this ridiculous hairdo and took off these blasted shoes—she
was climbing into bed and pulling the covers over her
head. If she was lucky, everyone would leave her alone
for the next twenty-four hours.

At the sound of a truck pulling alongside her, Abby

had the distinct feeling that her luck had taken a long vacation.

"Abby."

She ignored Callan's call and kept walking.

"Abby, get in the truck."

It was so blasted hard to be dignified in spiked heels, she thought, not to mention the skimpy clothing she had on. For Heaven's sake, she looked like a street-walker. She wondered what he'd do if she cocked her hip and asked him if he was looking for a date.

Somehow, she didn't think he'd see the humor in it.

When he jumped the curb at the next streetlight and slammed on his brakes, she gasped and took a step back. He threw open his door and stepped in front of her, his face dark and fierce. "Where in the hell do you think you're going?"

"There's a hooker convention at the women's club tonight," she said sweetly. "I thought I'd stop by and say hello."

He jammed a thumb toward his truck. "Get in. I'm taking you home."

"Thank you, but it's such a lovely night, I thought I'd walk." She attempted to move around him, but he blocked her way.

"Don't be ridiculous," he said tightly. "It's cold."

"Not at all." She tried not to shiver. "It's actually quite invigorating."

"You're freezing."

When his gaze dropped to her tight-fitting blouse, she realized it was quite obvious that she was, in fact, cold. Very cold. She covered her breasts with her arms, wondering if there would ever be an end to the embarrassment she'd already suffered tonight.

Obviously not, she thought, and gave a small squeak

as he scooped her up in his arms and carried her to his truck. He deposited her on the front seat, slammed the door and climbed back in behind the wheel.

Well, he certainly didn't need to act like a barbarian, Abby thought, though her pulse raced and her skin tingled from his touch. Lifting her chin and squaring her shoulders, she sat as primly as a woman dressed like The Happy Hooker possibly could.

Callan couldn't decide if he wanted to shake Abby or kiss her, though he suspected his bad mood was a combination of both. So for the short drive to her house, he felt it best to keep his hands tightly on the wheel and his gaze locked to the road. He'd barely pulled into the driveway and stopped the truck before she was sliding out of the cab and walking to her front door, though he decided that the word walking didn't quite apply to the sensuous sway of her hips and rear end. He didn't think that mankind had found an accurate word for that completely feminine movement, but he did know that its force equaled atomic proportions.

He watched her longer than was sensible or prudent, closed his eyes on a groan, then got out of the truck and caught up with her at the front door. Because she'd left her purse at the tavern, she stood there in the darkness, shoulders back and head high, waiting for him to open the door for her with the key she'd given him the first night he'd stayed at her house.

"I'd rather be alone tonight, Callan," she said after he unlocked the door.

"Fine." He swung the door open wide. "After we talk."

He saw the slight droop of her shoulders, and though his palms itched to touch her, he didn't dare.

That would be a big mistake.

"Would you like some coffee?" she asked with charm-school politeness after she turned on the living room lamp. "Or maybe a brandy? I believe I have a bottle somewhere."

"No, I don't want coffee or a brandy, dammit. I want to know what the hell that was all about back there."

"That was our engagement party."

He frowned darkly. "You know what I mean, Abby."

"If you're referring to my dance number," she said coolly, "it's traditional at my family's events for the guest, or guests, of honor to perform. You and I happened to be the unfortunate victims tonight. If I had known about the party, I would have warned you, but I didn't know. By the way, I think you have a very nice voice."

He rolled his eyes at her compliment. God help him, what the hell was he going to do with this woman?

Don't go there, Cal.

He pointed to the sofa. "Sit down, Abby."

Back straight, hands folded demurely in her lap, she sat on the edge of the sofa and met his gaze. He stood on the other side of the room, needing to keep some distance between them.

"I apologize if I've embarrassed you in front of your family and friends." Her words held all the starch of a preacher's collar.

"Embarrass me?" Shaking his head, he ran a hand through his hair. "Right now, I suspect I'm the envy of every man in Bloomfield County."

Her face turned nearly the same shade of red that was on her lips. "I didn't embarrass you?"

"Embarrass me?" He gave a dry laugh and shook

his head. "You surprised the hell out of me. God, Abby, you were amazing, unbelievable. There wasn't a man in the place who could take his eyes off you."

Including me, he thought. *Especially me.* And every other man who'd looked at her, including his brothers, he'd wanted to rip apart. Especially that Roberto guy. Just thinking about the way he'd touched Abby, the way she'd wrapped her legs around him at the end of the number, made his blood start to boil all over again.

On a groan, she dropped her head into her hands, as if his compliments were too much to bear. He sat beside her, confused by her reaction. "That upsets you?"

She nodded, keeping her face covered with her hands.

"I don't understand. You were terrific."

"I don't want to be terrific." Her bare shoulders rolled forward as she bent to take her heels off, setting them neatly on the floor. "Not at that. I never wanted that. Not when I was five or ten or fifteen. And most certainly not now."

He heard a sad weariness in her voice, saw a vulnerability in her that he'd never seen before. Wanting only to reassure her, he slipped an arm around her waist and tucked her against his chest. "What do you want, Abby?"

"The same thing I've always wanted. To be normal, to be like everyone else."

She wasn't like anyone else, Callan thought. She was the most amazing woman he'd ever met. But somehow he didn't think she wanted to hear that right now. "You don't think you're normal?"

She lowered her hands back to her lap and stared at them. "When other little girls were having tea parties and playing with dolls, I was either rehearsing or performing. Until I was sixteen, we moved and traveled so often, I just kept my clothes in a suitcase.''

Callan had spent a good portion of the past two years on the road, had lived out of his own suitcase. It was hard enough as an adult, but as a child? He was beginning to understand why she was so orderly, so precise and efficient. She simply wanted what she'd never had as a child—stability.

''And when you were sixteen?''

''My father ran off with a pretty, young understudy from *The King and I*.'' She looked up at him, her red lips set tight. ''To this day when I hear the word *et cetera* I want to punch something.''

''Maybe you should.'' He smiled at her. ''You might feel a whole lot better.''

''I don't think so,'' she said with sigh. ''I'd probably just end up feeling worse.'' She flipped open the top of the wooden birdhouse she kept on the end table beside her sofa, pulled out a tissue from the box hidden inside, then dabbed at her red lips.

''My mom and I went to live with Aunt Emerald and Ruby after my dad left. As you can imagine, living with my aunts was hardly what I'd call normal, but at least we never moved again. And I made everyone happy by performing in the drama class productions at school.''

''Everyone but yourself,'' he said evenly.

''I was happy living in the same house, going to the same school.'' She shrugged. ''That was good enough for me.''

''You shouldn't have to settle for good enough, Abby,'' he said thoughtfully. ''Did you ever tell them how you felt?''

''I wanted to, but after my mother got sick when I

was a senior, I just couldn't. It was too important to
her that I carry on the family tradition. I was in my
second year of college, theater arts major, when she
died.''

She stared at the red lipstick on the tissue, then
folded it neatly and set it on the coffee table.

''She was so proud.'' Abby dragged both hands
through her hair to smooth it down. ''So happy I had
the lead in the school's production of *Grease,* with
good enough reviews to land several offers for bigger
roles. I couldn't take that away from her. But after she
was gone, I saw no reason to continue. I finished my
commitment to the play, switched my major to business, then eventually took a job with a large accounting
firm.''

She looked up at him and smiled. ''You should have
seen the look on my aunts' faces when I told them.
You'd have thought that I'd joined a cult.''

He thought of Emerald and Ruby and smiled back
at her. ''I can imagine.''

Her smile faded. ''Unfortunately, that's when they
decided that if I wasn't going into show business, then
I needed a man to take care of me. For the next year
they brought home every available bachelor within a
hundred-mile radius. When they signed me up for that
television dating show, *The Perfect Match,* I decided
I'd had enough and moved into my own apartment in
New Jersey. When they started showing up there, too,
with men in tow, I knew I had to go somewhere they
wouldn't follow. Someplace quiet and small and far
enough away from the theater and nightlife they love
so much.''

''Bloomfield?''

She nodded. ''I'd been reading want ads in out-of-

town newspapers when I saw yours. 'Need hardwork-
ing, organized office manager with sharp mind, for
growing, busy construction company,'" she quoted
from memory. "'Only the best need apply.'"

She remembered the ad he'd placed? Good Lord,
he'd thought that by this time nothing Abby said or did
could amaze him more than she already had. And yet
she still did, almost as much as she fascinated him.

"Do you know what it's like to never fit in anywhere?" she asked softly. "To never feel that you be-
long? Working for you, in your office, made me feel
as if I was part of something important. Something
solid and permanent. I know that probably sounds silly
to you, but it's exactly what I was looking for, what I
wanted. This past year has been very special to me,
and I want to thank you for that."

Callan's gaze dropped to Abby's lips, lips that he'd
kissed only an hour ago. That he wanted to kiss again.

"It's not over," he murmured, ran his fingers over
her jaw, then splayed his fingers on her slim white
neck. So incredibly soft. "Not by a long shot."

Covering her mouth with his, he felt the shudder
move from her body to his. The ache that had been
slowly spreading through him quickened, then tightened as she parted her lips for him.

He deepened the kiss, was certain he'd never tasted
anything so sweet. So intoxicating. Her hands slid ten-
tatively up his chest, then around his neck. He crushed
her to him, groaned at the feel of her soft breasts
pressed against his chest. He felt her heart beating er-
ratically against his own; pleasure ripped through him,
as intense as it was endless.

When his mouth moved to her neck, her head fell
back in surrender. He blazed hot kisses down the long,

smooth column, tasted every dip and curve, felt the wild pounding of her pulse beside the hollow of her neck as he nipped her gently with his teeth.

She gasped at the scrape of his teeth on her skin, and her small whimper made his blood boil. He reined himself in, wanting to slow things down, to savor the taste and feel of her.

Shaken by the force of the need pumping through him, he put his hands on her shoulders and eased her away. "Abby," he said raggedly, "we're not pretending this time."

She opened her eyes slowly. They were deep-green, smoky and glazed with passion. It was all he could do not to take her that instant, hard and fast.

"What?" she murmured.

"This time it's real." He held her face in his hands, brushed his thumbs over her kiss-swollen lips. "This has nothing to do with your aunts or work or anything else. Do you understand? This is between you and me."

Her eyes widened as his words sank in. "You and me?"

He nodded. "You and me. If you don't want this, if you don't want me to make love to you, tell me now, before this goes any further."

Not want him to make love to her? Abby thought dimly. How could he possibly think that? Didn't he know, couldn't he see?

To please her aunts, she'd gone out on countless dates, and she couldn't remember even one of those faces, remember even one of their names. And though several had been nice enough, not one of them had ever made her feel like this. Not even close.

She almost laughed at the absurdity of his question. Of course she wanted him to make love to her!

But she wouldn't tell him that she wanted him more than her next breath. She would show him.

Sliding a hand behind his head, she tugged him toward her, brought his mouth back to hers.

On a moan he crushed her to him, and the feel of his hard, strong body against hers made her bones turn to taffy. She felt as if she were melting into the sofa as he pushed her back onto the soft cushions.

He kissed her like he'd never kissed her before, with a hunger that startled and excited at the same time. Her skin felt hot and cold, as if she'd been turned inside out, with every nerve exposed. He could kiss her like this forever, she thought.

Until his hands started to move.

And then she knew she wanted more. So much more.

His callused palms skimmed her bare shoulders, slid down her arms, where he linked his hands with hers, then raised them over her head. With her body pinned beneath his, she felt completely powerless, and yet somehow that aroused her beyond anything she could have ever imagined.

She was breathing hard when his mouth left hers and moved to nuzzle her earlobe, then trailed over her shoulder. Finally his lips made their way to the rise of her breast. She arched under him, impatient, biting her lip to hold back the groan hovering in her throat. Her skin felt tight and swollen and when he nipped gently at the soft flesh, she gasped. He used his teeth to tug her tight black top down, and she lay open to him, exposed.

When he took her in his mouth, she cried out.

He responded by laving her hardened nipple with his

hot, wet tongue. Like an arrow of fire, desire shot from the tip of her breast to the ache between her legs. Sensations too intense to control rolled through her like a tidal wave, and she shuddered from the force of them. When he moved to her other breast, she sucked in a sharp breath.

"I...I need to touch you," she gasped. "Please."

Keeping his attention on the tight, sensitive bud of her breast, he loosened his hold on her, slowly slid his roughened hands down the underside of her arms until he cupped her fully in his palms. Shivering, she dragged her fingers over his scalp, down his neck and shoulders, strained her body upward to fit more closely to his.

His mouth moved upward again, caressed the rise of her breast, then slid toward her neck. "Abby," he murmured, "that thing you did with your legs tonight, at the end of your dance, can you do that now?"

"Thing?" She struggled to understand his words, but her mind spun like a child's colorful top. She breathed in sharply as his thumbs stroked her nipples. "What thing?"

He slid his hands to her rear end, pulled the vee of her legs directly against the hard length of him. Blood pounded in her head, and the ache between her thighs became unbearable.

Oh, *that* thing.

She wrapped her legs tightly around him.

On a moan, he slid his arms around her and stood, then carried her to the bedroom.

He only bumped into two walls before they finally managed to tumble onto her bed.

Arms and bodies linked, laughing, they rolled together on the mattress. Never had she felt so incredibly alive, so aware of herself and everything around her. The thick cotton comforter against her back, the chirp of crickets outside her window, the masculine scent of Callan's skin.

The taste of desire.

A kaleidoscope of sensations washed over her, and she let herself be swept away in the rippling colors and textures. With Callan, she felt no inhibitions, no stage fright, no shyness. He made her feel what she'd never felt before, sexy and powerful and sure of herself. When he rolled her on top of him, she raised her arms and drew the tight band of black spandex over her head and tossed it away. He reared up, stroked her with his hands, his mouth, then they were rolling again.

Buttons flew, a zipper hissed in the darkness and then there was only bare skin against bare skin.

She'd waited for this all her life, waited for him. He moved over her; she slid her hands up his strong muscular arms. It made no difference she'd never done this before. Nothing could have felt more natural, more right.

Callan's breathing was hard and ragged as he crushed his lips to hers. She sucked in a breath at the brush of his thumbs over her nipples, and when his mouth moved down her neck and replaced his thumbs, she cried out. The urgency to have him inside her overwhelmed her. She slid her legs over his, then around his waist, pulling him closer.

''Abby.'' He gasped her name once, then again.

At the first press of velvet-steel, Abby wrapped her arms tightly around his shoulders and opened to him.

Callan hesitated at the resistance, lifted his head in confusion and looked at her. ''Wait, you—''

She dragged her mouth to his and surged upward, completely joining their bodies.

"Abby…dammit…hold on—"

"I am holding on," she murmured huskily, and started to move her hips.

On an oath his control broke. He thrust deeply, burying himself inside her.

Abby felt more pleasure than pain, but with that pleasure was an intense pressure, a desperate need that demanded release.

When it came, she fell apart, shattered into tiny, shimmering pieces. On a deep groan, he followed her.

"Abby, you could have told me."

He'd tucked her tightly against his body, held her close while he waited for the world to straighten again. He felt the beating of her heart against his chest and the warmth of her breath on his skin as she snuggled closer.

"I don't recall that particular question on my job application," she breathed. "Check appropriate box— virgin…nonvirgin."

How could she joke at a time like this? This was…important. "You know what I mean. Tonight. You should have told me tonight. Before things… escalated."

"And if I had told you?" she asked quietly. "What would you have done?"

Honest to God, he didn't know. "We should have at least discussed it."

She laughed at that, leaned her elbow on his chest and braced her head with her hand while she looked up at him. "All right. Let's discuss it now. Tell me about your previous sexual relations."

He frowned at her. "We aren't talking about me. We're talking about you."

She arched one eyebrow. "So you think that I should have discussed my sexual encounters, or lack of, with you, before we made love, but you, of course, wouldn't discuss yours with me."

He was getting her point, loud and clear, but that didn't mean he had to like it. "Don't twist this around, Abby. You're twenty-six years old. You told me you dated a lot of men. What was I supposed to think?"

She went still at his words, then said quietly, too quietly, "I don't know about the women you dated, but just because I went out with a lot of men, doesn't mean I slept around." She sat, covering herself with the sheet as she turned her back to him. "I think you'd better go."

God, he was an idiot. He'd certainly never meant to hurt her. That was the last thing he wanted.

"Abby." He ran his fingers up and down her arm, felt her shiver in spite of her anger. "I'm just a little off balance here. No, a *lot* off balance. Not just because you were a virgin, but because that was the single most incredible experience I've ever had in my life."

Her head came up, but she stayed where she was, her back stiff. "You're just saying that."

She resisted, but he tugged her back to him. "No, I'm not just saying that. I mean it."

Her eyes were bright with moisture as she looked at him. "Really?"

He took her index finger and made an *X* over his chest, felt his body respond to her touch. "Cross my heart."

Her lashes fluttered down. "It was for me, too," she whispered. "Incredible, I mean."

He brought her hand to his lips, kissed her knuckles. "It wouldn't have changed anything if you'd told me," he said with a sigh. "Nothing at all. I was foolish enough to think I could resist you, but the truth is, I've wanted you since the night you sat across the table from me in the tavern and told me that we were engaged. With your cheeks flushed and your glasses falling off, you were so damned cute I wanted to throw you over my shoulder and carry you out of there."

He was certain she was blushing, though it was too dark to tell. He touched her cheek, felt the heat on his fingertips.

"I've made such a fool of myself," she whispered.

He shook his head. "You wanted to make your aunts happy. That doesn't make you a fool. We wouldn't be here right now if it wasn't for them."

She smiled, lifted her gaze to his. "No, I don't suppose we would."

He cupped her chin in his hand, lowered his face to hers. "We should be thanking them both."

"Yes." Her lips parted as he moved closer. "I'll do that."

When her mouth brushed his, he felt the fire leap in his blood again. So soon, he thought in amazement. He was already aching and hard for her.

"Abby," he whispered, pulling her tightly against him. "That Roberto guy?"

Her breathing was shallow, her lips moist from his kiss. "What about him?"

"If he touches you again, I'll break him in half."

Before the laughter died in her throat, she was already moaning.

Eight

She woke slowly, a gradual ascent from the foggy depths of a dream. A wonderful, sexy dream about Callan that involved bare skin, slow, deep kisses and soft moans. Warm and cozy, she snuggled her cheek against her pillow and smiled.

Her smile froze when a callused palm skimmed over her hip.

Her bare hip.

Oh, dear.

As she opened her eyes slowly, the morning light glared at her. She felt the full length of Callan's body pressed against her back, burning her skin.

She swallowed hard and remembered.

Abby had never spent the night with a man before, which certainly made sense, since she'd never made love with a man before.

She smiled again.

Amazing. Absolutely amazing.

Was he awake? she wondered. And how was she supposed to act? Casual? Nonchalant? Composed? She supposed that most women were comfortable waking up next to a man they'd made love to most of the night. They just accepted it in stride, stretched, yawned, said good-morning.

Abby wanted to belt out a song.

It had to be the Bliss-Thomas blood in her, she thought and was so afraid she might start singing, she bit her tongue.

She wanted to dance, too. Right here on the bed. Dance and sing and laugh.

Burying her head in her pillow, she grinned broadly.

"Oh, What a Beautiful Mornin'" would be about right.

She didn't sing it out loud, just in her head.

"Abby, you awake?"

She jumped at Callan's soft call, unintentionally elbowing him in his ribs. He made a strangled *oomph* sound.

Horrified that she'd hurt him, she turned quickly. "I'm so sorry. Did I hurt you?"

He rubbed at his broad, powerful chest, then a slow grin spread over his sleepy, incredibly handsome face as he stared at her.

"You could kiss it," he suggested.

Heat poured through her body. Her *naked* body.

Dear Lord, they were both naked. In bed. In the light of day. His hand slid over her hip.

She forced the song out of her head. "Ah, Callan, I don't want you to think—"

His arms came around her, and he dragged her closer. "I don't want you to think, either, Abby."

And then he was kissing her senseless. Wrapping her arms around his neck, she kissed him back, lost herself in the feel of his skin against hers.

When he finally drew back, she was breathless and more than a little aroused. She opened her eyes slowly, met his dark, amused gaze.

She smiled.

He smiled back.

"I'm not sure what to do here," she said hesitantly. "This is a first for me."

Pleasure shone in his eyes at her honest statement. "You're supposed to tell me I'm wonderful, cook me a big breakfast, then serve it in bed."

Amazed, she realized that he was teasing. "Oh, is that the agenda? Well, you were wonderful." She bit her lip and stared thoughtfully over his shoulder. "Though I am a novice myself, so I can't really say for sure."

He raised a brow at that. "Well, I *am* wonderful. In fact, last night you told me so. Several times."

She felt her cheeks burn. "I said that?"

"Well, not in words." His hands moved down her back, slid over her rear end and lingered there. "But they say actions always speak louder than words."

He cupped her buttocks in his palms and kneaded. She sucked in a breath. "Is that what they say?"

"Yep." His lips nibbled at her ear, then her neck.

Struggling to breathe, she found her own hands moving restlessly over his arms and chest. "Did you ever wonder who 'they' are?"

"Nope."

When his lips closed over the hardened peak of one breast, Abby ceased to wonder herself. She arched toward him, digging her fingers into his scalp at the sweet, wonderful feel of his wet, warm tongue on her sensitive nipple. Her head fell back on a moan.

"Callan," she gasped, "please."

And then he did. Completely.

Callan thought he had to be the luckiest man alive.

He could only imagine the stupid grin he had on his face at the moment, but he didn't give a damn. He'd just had the most incredible night of his life, and at this very moment he was holding the most incredible woman in his arms.

Lying on his back, he stroked Abby's soft hair, fascinated by its silken texture. Her hair was only one of her exceptional assets that she'd kept hidden for the past year, he thought. She had several other qualities of notable mention. Just thinking about those qualities made him hard all over again.

She'd dozed off after they'd made love, and he could still see the flush of passion on her skin. But as badly as he wanted to make love with her again, he would let her sleep for while. God knew they certainly hadn't gotten much sleep last night.

His grin widened.

Yes, sir. He was one lucky son of a gun.

He could have it all—Abby and the best secretary in the world.

Why hadn't he seen it before? They were both mature, reasonable adults. There was no reason they couldn't work together, be completely professional with each other during the day and lovers at night.

He wasn't sure what Abby was thinking, but he wasn't going to let her think for a while. She might try to overrationalize the situation. Once she had a little time to let the idea sink in, to accept that they were capable of a relationship both in and out of the office, then she'd see how simple it all would be. How easy.

How perfect.

For the weekend, though, he intended to keep her mind and body occupied. Monday morning, after they'd spent two days together, he would discuss it with her. But not before.

She would see things his way.

Murmuring, she stirred in his arms, and he pressed a kiss to her temple. Damn, but she felt good. Soft and warm.

Her hands moved slowly over his chest, downward, under the sheet, and he felt the fire jumping in his veins.

They could sleep later, he decided.

He rolled her to her back, watched her eyes slowly open as she looked at him through passion-heavy lids. He moved over her, felt her arms curl around his neck and pull him closer—

The doorbell rang.

"My aunts!" Abby's face turned white. "They told me last night that they were coming over this morning."

Ice water wouldn't have brought them out of the bed as quickly as the insistent *bing-bong* of her doorbell. Abby scrambled for something to cover herself with, but the clothes she'd worn home from the tavern last night weren't exactly what she wanted to wear to greet her aunts. She snatched the comforter from where it had fallen onto the floor during the night, wrapped it around herself and stumbled to her closet. Callan reached for his jeans and dragged them on.

"I'll let them in," he said, and tugged up his zipper.

"No!" She spun, a robe clutched in her fingers.

"Abby." He took her chin in his hand. "We had an engagement party last night. Ruby and Emerald think I live here. I don't think we're going to shock them."

She stared at him, eyes wide. "But—"

"No buts." He pressed a kiss to her nose. "I'll make some coffee, and we'll visit for a few minutes. Now stop worrying and get dressed."

The doorbell rang again, and she glanced nervously toward the front of the house, then looked back at him. She sucked in a long breath and nodded slowly.

"Good girl."

He hurried to the guest bedroom and grabbed a blue T-shirt from his bag and was still pulling it on as he opened the front door.

Emerald and Ruby stood on the other side of the door, dressed in their usual layers of brightly colored gauze. Together they chirped, "Good morning."

They bustled inside, carrying Abby's purse and clothes from the night before, asking if she was feeling better. He assured them she was fine, and while he made coffee, they gave detailed accounts of the guests activities at the party the night before.

Miss Rose Primple, the librarian at Bloomfield High School, performed "Second-hand Rose."

The mayor sang "Jailhouse Rock" and gave a pulsating-pelvis imitation of the "The King" that brought the house down.

And Lucian, of all people, his most reticent brother, gave his own rendition of George Thoroughgood's "Bad to the Bone." Callan would have given a month's pay to see that. He could only imagine that his younger brother had one hell of a hangover today.

If nothing else, Callan thought, as he poured coffee for Emerald and Ruby, the two women had definitely brought a little life to Bloomfield, and he would miss them.

But even though they certainly knew how to have fun and liven up a party, Callan couldn't imagine living in the same house with them, never being able to catch your breath or your balance. He thought about what Abby had told him last night, how she'd never fit in with her family's lifestyle. And though she obviously had the talent, and most likely could be a star, she wanted a regular-hours, same-work-every-day office job.

And she was all his. In every way.

He smiled. *The luckiest man alive.*

"Good morning, dear," Emerald and Ruby said at the same time.

Callan turned, watched as Abby walked hesitantly into the kitchen. She'd pulled on a long, soft-pink cotton dress, brushed her hair back and clipped it with pearl barrettes over her ears. She kissed her aunts good-morning, then glanced at him, a mixture of shy and coquette that stirred his blood, made him anxious to be alone with her again.

"Feeling better?" Emerald asked as Abby pulled a mug out of the cupboard.

"Much, thank you." Callan saw the blush on her cheeks before she turned to the coffeepot. "It was just a headache. I'm fine now."

"Abby." Ruby patted the chair beside her. "Come sit, dear. You, too, Callan. Auntie Emerald and I would like to speak with you both."

Abby spilled coffee over the sides of the cup she'd been filling. Her gaze shot like a bullet toward Callan, but he just shrugged and waved a hand toward the table. Shoulders stiff, Abby sank down onto a chair. Callan was certain she wasn't even breathing.

"We want you both to know we've had a wonderful time this week," Ruby said. "But we've decided to leave for Florida a few days early and take in the Miami sights."

"You're leaving?" Abby had a blank look on her face.

"Today, if you don't mind terribly." Emerald patted her niece's hand. "We have a taxi waiting to take us to the airport now."

"But you—"

"We'll be back for the wedding, of course," Ruby reassured her. "Let us know the minute you set the date."

When Abby started to protest, Emerald shushed her. "Now, now, dear, you know how we hate goodbyes. So just give us a hug, and we'll call you when we get back to New York."

They both stood, pulled Abby to her feet, then hugged her in turn. Callan found himself enclosed in their arms next, and they each kissed him soundly on his cheek.

"We'll miss you both." Emerald patted Callan on his cheek and looked up at him with a smile. "Take good care of her, Callan. She's a jewel."

They blew out as they'd blown in, even gave them a few verses from a song out of *Gypsy* when Abby and Callan walked them to the front door.

The silence fell, heavy and awkward, when the door closed behind them. Hands clasped in front of her, Abby shifted from one foot to the other. "Well," she finally said. "I guess that's that."

He moved toward her. "What's what?"

She cleared her throat. "You know, *that*. You don't have to…stay."

"Do you want me to leave, Abby?"

Her gaze lifted, leveled with his. "No."

Thank God. He released the breath he'd been holding, then took her face in his hand and brushed his lips over hers, felt complete satisfaction at the shudder that moved through her body.

She smiled softly, then took his hand and led him back to her bed.

The luckiest man alive.

After the most incredible weekend of her life, it wasn't easy for Abby to settle back into work on Monday. The fact that Callan had been out on the Palmer job site since early that morning should have made it less difficult, but she had taken twice as long to type up a breakdown on the Waterman project, she'd made two errors on the month's spreadsheet and she'd nearly forgotten to order the insurance certificates for the remodel Gabe was working on.

Worse still, she'd caught herself daydreaming at least a dozen times.

And, God help her, she'd been humming all day. Had to bite her tongue several times to keep herself from singing out loud.

She and Callan had yet to discuss what had happened between them the past two days and what it meant. Over the weekend, every time she'd attempted to broach the subject of work, he'd quickly distracted her.

Much to her embarrassment, she'd been easy to distract.

At the memory of how much she'd enjoyed those

distractions, her cheeks warmed. And other, more intimate, parts of her anatomy ached.

Every touch, every sigh, every moan, came back to her, and her skin burned. He'd been an incredible lover, what every woman fantasized about. Attentive and gentle one moment, forceful and strong the next. She'd barely caught her breath all weekend.

She could barely catch it now.

But it was Monday. Her aunts had left on Saturday, and the weekend, as wonderful as it had been, was behind her.

There was no reason to pretend any longer.

She blinked back the threatening tears. She wouldn't cry. She wouldn't. The past two days with Callan had been more wonderful than she ever could have dreamed. She refused to regret even one minute. But she had to face reality now, face the fact that she'd made love with Callan. And a situation that had been improbable before, now became impossible.

With a heavy sigh, she tucked a loose strand of hair into the bun at the base of her neck and forced her attention back to her computer screen. She needed to finish typing up her releases for payments to subcontractors by the end of the day. At the rate she was working, she wouldn't be finished for two weeks.

She'd almost typed one half of a payment when the door opened and Callan walked in. She soaked in the all-male sight of him: worn denim covered his long, powerful legs; a navy-blue flannel shirt, sleeves rolled up to expose muscular forearms; thick work boots encased his large feet. Everything about him was big, she thought, and felt a blush work its way up her neck.

And when he smiled at her, her entire body felt soft and warm.

"Hi." His voice was husky; his gaze locked on her mouth.

Exactly the way he'd woken her up this morning, she thought.

Remembering what had happened *after* he'd woken her up, she jumped up and grabbed a large brown envelope sitting on her desk and held it in front of her as if it were a shield.

"Hello." She cleared her throat. "The soils report from the Waterman project is on your desk along with the breakdown for the subcontractors, a set of blueprints from the architect on the New Jersey development, and you have a voice message from your sister."

He moved toward her with intent in his eyes. She backed toward the file cabinet.

"Oh, and Mr. Palmer's secretary called a few minutes ago. He changed his flight from two in the afternoon to eleven in the morning. She hopes that won't be a problem for you picking him up at the airport."

"No problem at all."

Damn, but she was cute, Callan thought as he watched Abby fidget. All neat and tidy and conservative in her usual business attire. He'd never thought those suits sexy before, but now, hell, after their weekend together, her starched look just made him want to unbutton her jacket and mess her up.

He'd intentionally stayed out of the office longer than necessary today, just to give her a little time alone. He knew that it was going to be awkward for her at first, working with him and sleeping together, too, but she'd get used to the idea. It was just a matter of time and patience on his part.

He could see she was flustered, that she was struggling to maintain a professional façade. She held a large mailing envelope in her hands with a death grip, and she was stiff as a post. It gave him tremendous satisfaction that he unnerved the fastidiously efficient Abigail Thomas.

And he wanted to do so much more.

But the time had come to discuss their…situation. And since she was probably feeling a little too timid to bring it up, he'd make the first move to put her at ease.

"Abby—"

"Callan, we need to talk." She lifted her chin, firmly met his gaze. "Could we please go in your office?"

"Huh? Oh, sure." He gestured for her to go first, closed the door behind them. He still had his hand on the doorknob when she turned to face him.

"Abby—"

"I just want you to know how much I appreciate what you did for me. I don't know how to ever thank you."

Since Callan knew that Abby was much too reserved to bring up the subject of their lovemaking, she was obviously talking about the engagement masquerade. "You don't need to thank me, Abby. I enjoyed meeting your aunts. They're terrific ladies."

"They think you're terrific, too." She stared down at the envelope she still clutched in her hand, then drew in a slow breath and looked back up at him. "And so do I."

He smiled at her. Now they were getting somewhere. This was the perfect time to discuss their own situation, though he knew he needed to choose his words carefully and not mention how great the sex had been between them and how much he enjoyed being with her the past two days. He didn't want to embarrass her.

"Abby—"

"I also want you to know how wonderful this past weekend was for me," she said before he could continue. "You were a wonderful, incredible lover. You made me feel things I didn't know I was capable of feeling."

Her eyes fluttered downward. He blinked at her, too stunned that she'd brought the subject up to even feel smug or proud. She might be dressed like a puritan, but she certainly wasn't talking like one.

Damn if it didn't turn him on.

He felt himself grow hard. He wanted her right now. Right here. His blood pumped fierce and hot in his veins. He glanced at his desk, noted that it was cluttered with paperwork. One swipe of his arm could take of that, he decided.

"...always be grateful, but I'm sure you see how things are different now."

He stopped midstride on the way to his desk. He'd lost part of what she'd said, and something told him he needed to stop thinking with the lower part of his anatomy and listen to what she was saying.

"The agency assures me that they have a competent replacement, and they'll send her out first thing in the morning."

"Replacement?" His head whipped up. "What replacement?"

"I just said that the agency—"

"Never mind about the agency. *What* replacement?"

"Mine, of course. I just explained that."

His eyes narrowed as he moved toward her. "Explain it again."

Her shoulders squared, but she didn't back away when he inched in close. She lifted her chin, hugged that damn envelope even tighter. "I can't work here now, Callan. Not after what happened between us this weekend. Surely you can understand that."

Hell, he hadn't understood one thing that had happened to him since he'd come back from Woodbury and found Francine sitting at Abby's desk. Why would this be any different? "No, I *don't* understand. Why can't you work here?"

Her cheeks turned bright pink. "Because we...we slept together."

Crazy. This was absolutely crazy. He'd pretended he was engaged to her while her aunts were here, done cartwheels and handstands to keep her, and now she was leaving anyway? Because they'd slept together?

He'd expected her to try and distance herself from him now that her aunts were gone, but he certainly hadn't expected her to *quit*.

God help him, would he *ever* understand women?

"What happened this weekend," he said carefully, "has nothing to do with our work. I admit I might get distracted from time to time, but we're adults, Abby. We can certainly refrain from any lascivious displays of lust in the office. And what we do at night—" he leaned in closer, brought his mouth within a whisper of hers "—nobody needs to know but us."

She nearly leaned toward him, then blinked quickly and pulled back. "*I* would know, Callan. Sex in the office never works."

"We've never had sex in the office," he said evenly and looked at his desk. "But we could test the theory."

Her entire face colored now. "That's not what I

meant. I'm talking about office flings. They don't work.''

Fling? He wasn't sure if he wanted to shake her or kiss her, but since neither one was a good idea, he shoved his hands into his pockets. ''And how do you know that?''

''I pulled up some articles from the Internet. Saucy, Blaze and Sophistication. They all advised against it. Sleeping with your boss only leads to difficulties.''

''Let me get this straight,'' he said between clenched teeth. ''You're quitting because of an article you read in a magazine?''

''Of course not. They just confirmed what I was already feeling. I'd like us to be friends, but if I stay here, sooner or later what happened between us might happen again, and that would only lead to complications.''

Complications? His whole life had been nothing but complications since Abby's aunts had come into town. He could handle complications, dammit.

A deep, strangled sound rattled inside his throat. He took hold of her arms and yanked her to him. ''I'm not letting you quit, Abby. We'll work this out.''

He couldn't tell her he wouldn't make love to her again, because that would be a bald-faced lie, and she would know it. He wanted to make love to her right now. And tonight. Tomorrow and the day after that, too.

And he wanted her to work for him, too.

He refused to accept that he couldn't have both. She was just as attracted to him as he was to her. Even now he could see the desire in her eyes, the soft parting of her lips. And as much as he wanted to crush his mouth against hers, he realized this would be bad timing.

She just needed a little more time. He would convince her. She couldn't refuse him forever. She'd come around.

"Let's talk about this over dinner," he said gently, and loosened his hold on her.

She pushed the envelope she'd been holding into his arms. "No, Callan. I won't change my mind. I'll be in the office until next Monday, then I'll be gone. I'm sorry."

She moved around him and without looking back, left his office and closed the door quietly behind her. He swore under his breath, then looked in the envelope she'd given him.

Her resignation.

He felt something else in the envelope and looked inside. He pulled out the engagement ring and glared at it.

Damn you, Abigail Thomas!

He'd done absolutely everything he could think of to keep the woman. What the hell else could she possibly want?

On a growl, he ripped the envelope in two and dumped it in the trash can.

Resign? he thought angrily. I don't think so, Abby.

Nine

―――

"**A**re you avoiding me?"

Callan stared at his sister, considered shutting his
apartment door in her pretty little face. He sighed instead and stepped aside, letting her flounce past him in
her long, flowery skirt and white tank top.

"I left two messages on your phone here over the
weekend and two today on your voice mail at the office." Cara nearly stumbled over the open duffel bag
he'd tossed into the living room. Actually, he'd *thrown*
the bag against the wall when he'd come home a few
minutes ago, then kicked it. Several articles of clothing,
a can of shaving cream and tube of toothpaste lay scattered on the floor.

"I've been busy," he grumbled. "This isn't a good
time, Cara."

"Neither have the past three days, obviously." Fold-ing her arms, she stood in the middle of the living room and faced him. "What's going on, Cal?"

As much as he loved his sister, Callan was in no mood to go rounds with another stubborn female. He headed to the refrigerator, rooted for a beer, then swore when the best he could come up with was a diet orange soda.

"What makes you think there's something going on?" He popped the soda can open, sniffed at it. "Everything's just fine. Peachy, in fact."

She glanced at the mess on the floor, then looked back at him with one brow raised. "I can tell."

"A man's got a right to a little privacy, Cara." He swung the can in a wide gesture. "He should be able to come and go without anybody checking up on him and poking into his affairs, don't you think?"

Cara's raised brow arched higher. "Absolutely."

"Damn straight."

"So did you and Abby have a fight?"

He choked on the swig of soda in his mouth. "Fight? Abby doesn't fight. She makes logical, rational, *sensible* decisions based on articles in *Blaze.*"

"Abby reads *Blaze?*"

He dragged a hand through his hair. "Just the one about—" he started to say sex, then caught himself "—relationships in the office."

Cara nodded. "Oh, yeah, I read that one. It said that office flings were a bad idea and you should never sleep with your boss. Good article."

Flings. There was that damn word again. Abby wasn't a *fling,* dammit. "What the hell do they know?"

"Statistics," she said with a nod of her head. "It's exciting for a while, then it all falls to pieces, your job and your heart."

"She quit, dammit!" He slammed the soda on the coffee table and orange liquid sloshed out. "Just because we—"

"You slept together?" she finished the sentence for him when he hesitated.

Great. The last thing in the world he wanted was to discuss his sex life with his sister, of all people.

"That's nobody's business but ours." He thought of the mess it would make if he kicked the can of soda. It would almost be worth it. "She didn't have to quit. We're both adults. We could discuss it."

"I can imagine how you would *discuss* it, Cal." Cara sighed. "You want it all, don't you? Sex *and* the secretary. So like a man."

He frowned at her. She made it sound so…tacky. It wasn't like that at all. "Speaking of men, don't you have one to go home to?"

She smiled. "He's scouting a location for a new center in Trenton and won't be back until day after tomorrow. You have my full attention."

"Well, take it somewhere else, Sis. I don't want it or need it." What he wanted—what he *needed*—he couldn't have.

And that was Abby.

Cara laughed, actually *laughed* at him.

"This is priceless," she said between giggles. "For twenty-seven years I couldn't sneeze without my four big brothers saying gesundheit. And then that little incident six months ago, before Ian and I got married, when the four of you were spying on me? I don't recall needing or wanting your so-called help then, either."

She walked toward him and hugged him. He simply glared at her. "But you know what, big brother? As much as it annoyed me, it also made me feel good to know how much I was loved.''

How could she do that? he wondered. Make him so damn mad one minute, then make his gut twist the next. Sighing, he slipped his arms around her.

Women.

And there was another woman who could do that to him, he realized. One that he had absolutely no brotherly feelings for.

''Abby's not the type to take love lightly,'' Cara said and looked up into her brother's surprised eyes. ''She's going to need more than you're offering. If you can't give it to her, then you need to let her go.''

Love? Callan stared at his sister. Who said anything about love? He thought Abby was terrific, but he sure as hell wasn't ready for *that*. That was *way* down the road somewhere. He felt a chill shiver up his spine at the same time his heart slammed against his chest.

How did his sister know what type Abby was, anyway? He'd known her for a year, and he hadn't a clue. She had so many layers to her, so many different facets, she made his head swim. And he was certain there were more, waiting to be discovered. By him.

Let her go? He couldn't do that.

''I can see you're not listening to me,'' she said with a sigh, then touched his cheek. ''I'm meeting our brothers at the tavern. Wanna join me?''

He shook his head. He sure as hell didn't need his brothers' ribbing right now. ''You go on. Maybe I'll join you later.''

She smiled. ''Don't make me have to track you down next time. I need to know you're all right.''

''I'm fine, Sis.'' He kissed her cheek, slipped an arm around her shoulders and walked her to the door. ''I think I'm capable of handling this...situation on my own.''

She was halfway out the door when she turned to him. There was something in her eyes he couldn't read, but he remembered his mother called it ''the devil dancing'' look.

''Think again, Cal.'' A smile lightly touched her lips. ''And don't stand close to any cliffs.''

He closed the door behind her and frowned. Cliffs? What the hell was she talking about?

Abby stood at the kitchen sink, grating carrots for a salad, thinking about all the things she needed to do this evening: fold the clothes she'd put in the dryer when she got home from work, sort through three days' worth of mail, empty the trash for pickup tomorrow, wash the bathroom floor.

Decide what to do with the rest of her life.

She'd bought three different newspapers on her way home from work. Since she'd be needing a new job next week, she thought she should at least start looking at the employment opportunities. She wasn't in any special hurry: she'd put enough money aside these past few years that she didn't have to work for a while if she didn't want to. But she'd always felt more comfortable when she had a goal, a plan.

And the last thing she needed right now was time on her hands.

She knew that Callan was upset with her, and she certainly didn't blame him. She was upset with herself. That silly charade to fool her aunts, and it was all for nothing.

Well, not completely for nothing. A rush of heat coursed through her as she thought about her weekend with Callan. That never would have happened if they hadn't pretended to be engaged. And no matter what, she would never regret making love with Callan.

And she'd never regret falling in love with him, either.

When she first realized how she really felt about him, she'd denied it, of course. Told herself that she'd confused *making* love with *being* in love. That it was just an infatuation.

But she knew better. If nothing else, she was being honest with herself to admit that she was, in fact, in love with him.

Hopelessly, deeply in love.

At the sound of the doorbell, she dropped the grater, and it clattered into the sink. Her heart pounded in her chest as she wiped her hands on a towel and walked to the front door.

Please don't let it be Callan.

She was too vulnerable right now. She'd do something foolish if it was him. Something insane.

Something wonderful.

And still she was disappointed when she opened the door and it wasn't him. She was also surprised.

"Cara?"

"Hi." Callan's sister held a bouquet of red roses. "Mind if I come in?"

"Oh, of course. I'm sorry." Abby stepped aside to let her pass, caught the fragrant scent of the flowers. "Those are lovely."

Were they from Callan? Abby wondered and her pulse skipped.

"I bought them for you." Cara moved into the kitchen. "Do you have something to put them in?"

Hoping that the disappointment wasn't too evident

on her face, Abby opened the cupboard under the sink and pulled out a cut-crystal vase. "You brought me flowers?"

Cara unwrapped the clear plastic holding the flowers together, then arranged them in the vase. "I hope I didn't catch you at a bad time."

"No, ah, I was just grating some carrots."

When the vase was filled with water, Cara set them on the counter and turned to face Abby. "Cal told me you quit."

Abby felt the blood drain from her face. "Well, yes. I turned in my resignation today."

"Why?"

The same blood that had drained away now shot back up her neck to her cheeks. "I...well...I—"

"Abby," Cara said with a smile. "I'm the younger sister of four brothers. I had to learn early in life to say whatever it was I needed to say in the shortest time possible or I might not get a second chance."

How different their lives and families had been, Abby thought with envy. She'd always hated being an only child. "I just thought that it wasn't... appropriate."

"Because you slept together?"

Abby felt her breath catch. Was Callan already talking about what had happened between them? And how many other people had he told? "Did he—Callan tell you that?"

"You two disappeared after your performance on Friday night—which, by the way, was amazing," Cara added. "Then my brother doesn't return any of my messages for three days, which isn't like him at all."

Cara folded her arms and leaned back against the counter. "Before I got married and went to work for my husband's foundation, I used to be a private investigator, did you know that? My skilled and uncanny powers of observation figured out exactly why Callan was too busy to answer my calls.''

''Oh.'' Abby put a hand to her throat and closed her eyes.

''Just like I figured out that you're in love with him.''

Her eyes flew open. ''I'm not.''

Cara tilted her head and arched one brow. ''I saw the way you looked at him, Abby. From one woman in love to another, you most certainly are in love.''

Oh, what was the point in denying it? If nothing else, Abby found Cara's in-your-face manner a refreshing change from her own uptight attitude. Maybe it would feel good to tell someone the truth for a change. She drew in a deep breath. ''Yes, I am.''

Cara smiled. ''Now we're getting somewhere. So why did you quit?''

She glanced longingly at the roses, reached out and touched one velvet-soft petal. ''How could I be formal and polite and detached during the day, then sleep with him at night? That might sound old-fashioned, but to me it would feel…cheap.''

''He's in love with you, too, Abby.''

Her pulse jumped at the very thought. She shook her head slowly. ''It's just sex,'' she said quietly. ''As wonderful as it is between us, it's not enough for me. I couldn't survive an—'' she paused, then said quietly ''—affair.''

''I know Cal,'' Cara said firmly. ''And I know the look. He's in love with you, all right, he just doesn't know it. He's pacing his apartment like a crazed animal right now, thinking he's lost you, but he's not quite bright enough to know what to do about it. What can I say?'' she shrugged. ''He's a man.''

Abby might have laughed if her heart wasn't aching. Callan most certainly was a man, she thought, and the memory of his hands on her body, his lips on hers, stirred the heat of desire in her blood.

Cara rubbed her hands together. ''So how much time do we have?''

''Time?'' Abby frowned. ''Time for what?''

''When is your last day at work?''

''Monday. That's seven more days.''

Cara narrowed her eyes thoughtfully. ''We'll have to move ahead to the accelerated plan.''

''Accelerated plan?''

''I'll explain later.'' She picked up the stub of a carrot. ''You see this? That's what we're going to do to Cal. Grate him down to a nub until there's nothing left.''

Grate him down? She stared at the carrot, then looked at Cara. ''I don't understand why you're doing this.''

''Three reasons.'' She snatched up a fresh carrot and took a bite. ''One is payback for every time that Callan and my other brothers decided I needed advice or assistance in my life. The other is because I love Cal, and I want to see him happy. If I didn't believe that you were the woman for the job, I wouldn't be here.''

Cara took another bite of carrot and grinned. ''And the third reason is that we are going to have a ton of fun watching my brother go slowly crazy.''

Abby smiled. She was beginning to like the plan almost as much as she liked Cara.

Cara glanced at her watch. ''We've only got about three hours. Grab your purse and let's go.''

"Go? Go where?"

"Shopping, my dear." Cara slipped an arm around Abby's shoulders. "We're going shopping."

"Thirty-five years ago, when a man asked for finish-grade oak, he got finish-grade oak. These days I wouldn't build a doghouse with the so-called high-quality wood these suppliers think they can pawn off on a builder." Ray Palmer waved a thick-knuckled finger at the pretty redheaded waitress who'd brought their first round of drinks, and she hurried over.

"Another scotch and soda." Ray looked at his son, Jack, then Callan. "You boys ready for another round?"

Callan shook his head. He'd been so busy watching the restaurant doorway, he'd barely touched his beer. He glanced toward the entrance now, feeling as if the tie he'd put on with his black dress shirt was strangling him.

"I'm fine, Dad." Jack reached for the glass of red wine he'd been sipping.

When the waitress left, Ray glanced around the room and nodded at the dark woods, big beams and red tablecloths. "Nice joint you picked out, Sinclair. Reminds me of the steak houses I used to go to on the South side. Those were the days."

"Actually, Abigail made the reservations."

Just saying her name made his throat tighten. He hadn't gone into the office today, partly because he'd been busy out at the site with Ray and his son, partly because he reasoned that if he gave her a day to settle down, to rethink her resignation, she would come to the realization she belonged exactly where she was.

And if he were really honest with himself, he was

afraid to be alone with her right now. He knew he'd have to touch her, to kiss her, to slip that long straight skirt she always wore up over her thighs and—

"Yep, Abigail sure knows how to pick 'em," Ray interrupted Callan's wayward thoughts. "You're one lucky dog to have that little lady working for you, Sinclair. It's damn hard to find good help these days. So when does she get here? I can't wait to meet her."

Callan glanced at the doorway again. Abby was late, and Abby was *never* late. But when Ray had insisted she be invited tonight and Callan had called her at the office, she'd said she'd come. He didn't believe she wouldn't show.

But then, he didn't know what to think about Abby anymore. She had him twisted ten different ways.

"She should be here any minute." Callan reached for his beer. He hadn't told Ray about Abby quitting, nor did he intend to. Because she wasn't going to quit. He wouldn't let her. "If you'd like to go ahead and order—"

"Hell, no." Ray frowned. "My late wife, Isabel, taught me a few things about women. One is they like to make an entrance. Gives us men something to look forward to. Isn't that right, son?"

"Right, Dad." Jack swirled the glass of wine in his hand. "My father's got a thing for your secretary, Callan. You better keep an eye on her while he's around or he might snatch her away from you."

Teeth set tight, Callan forced a smile. Jack Palmer didn't look at all like his short, plump, balding father. Probably around thirty, Jack was at least six-two, with black, thick, wavy hair and piercing blue eyes that seemed to take everything in. Armani suit, Italian shoes, silk tie. Callan kept expecting him to say, "Bond. James Bond."

It wasn't that he didn't like the guy, Callan thought. He was pleasant enough, even though he didn't talk much. There was just something about him that…well, that he didn't like.

Maybe it was the crack about stealing Abby away, Callan decided. He *knew* he didn't like that comment one little bit.

Jack was lifting his glass when he suddenly went still. Callan glanced over his shoulder to follow the man's gaze.

His heart jumped into his throat.

Abby?

She floated toward them, dressed in a tight black halter dress that skimmed the top of her knees and hugged every luscious curve of breast and hip. Her stockings and high heels were black, too, her legs endless.

And her hair. He blinked. What on earth had she done to her hair? It fell in a sort of layered curtain around her face, emphasizing her big, smoky-green eyes. Eyes that were locked on him at the moment.

Where was the conservative suit she always wore? The pulled-back hair and glasses? This was a business dinner, he thought irritably. She should be dressed more…well, she should just be dressed more.

Not like a hot, sexy mama.

When his heart dropped back down into his chest, it started pumping as if he'd run three miles.

She smiled as she approached, a soft, enticing smile that made sweat pop out on his forehead. He jumped up, bumping the table as he stood. Ray and Jack stood, as well, both men clearly captivated.

"I hope you haven't been waiting long," she said smoothly, almost a purr, Callan thought. She extended her hand to Ray. "Mr. Palmer, a pleasure to finally meet you."

Even in the dim light of the restaurant, Callan could see Ray's face darken with a blush as he insisted she call him Ray. When she turned to Jack he took her hand and held it longer than necessary. Callan felt a hot pressure in his skull.

At least it hadn't been necessary to make introductions, Callan thought with annoyance. His tongue felt like a pretzel at the moment, anyway, and he probably would have just embarrassed himself. He was reaching to pull out her chair, but Ray beat him to it. When she sat, three pairs of male eyes dropped to the slit on the side of her dress and were treated with a brief glimpse of thigh before she scooted under the table.

Jack kept his gaze on Abby while Ray quickly signaled the waitress again. Callan clenched and unclenched his jaw, then took a long pull on his beer while she ordered a glass of white wine.

"Thank you for inviting me, Ray. I've been looking forward to meeting you and Jack." She picked up her napkin and folded it smoothly over her lap.

Callan drained his beer. Damn if he didn't want to be that napkin.

She smelled the way she looked, too. Something exotic and sexy that made him lean closer to pull her scent into his lungs.

"I want to compliment you on your taste, young lady," Ray said as soon as he seemed to catch his breath. "Those tile samples you sent to my office were exactly what I was looking for. They were a little on the high end, but the quality was first class. It's hard to find that kind of excellence these days.''

"You're absolutely right, Ray." Abby nodded. "I found some samples that were more economical, but I knew you were the kind of man who was willing to pay whatever price necessary for something that will last a lifetime."

Ray sat a little straighter in his chair. Jack watched Abby, a smile on his lips that made Callan's gut tighten. He knew what Ray's son was thinking. Exactly the same thing that *he* was thinking. Which was why he wanted to punch his lights out.

Callan wanted to feast on Abby without anyone else around: on the smooth curve of her shoulder, the rise of her breast, the slender column of her neck. He'd touched her in all those places, kissed her. He remembered what she felt like when he slipped inside her, how tight and hot and silky—

He jerked his mind back to the present, struggled not to glare at Jack Palmer for staring at Abby. Struggled not to take her by the arm and drag her out of the restaurant, yell at her for whatever it was she was doing to him, then make crazy love to her all night.

But because he couldn't do any of that, because he couldn't even touch her, let alone make love to her, he ordered another beer and watched her smile at Ray and Jack.

It was going to be one hell of a long night.

Ten

It wasn't easy to be a femme fatale, Abby decided three days later. Extra time with the hair and makeup, shorter skirts and lower-cut tops. High heels instead of her practical pumps.

And *garter belts,* of all things. Cara had pressured her into buying silk stockings that required garter belts. As she sat at her desk, working at her computer, she could feel the slide of black satin against her thighs.

No, it wasn't easy being a femme fatale, but Abby had to admit it certainly did feel wonderful.

When the phone rang, she picked it up. "Sinclair Construction."

"It's Day Four of 'Operation Callan,'" Cara said on the other end of the phone. "I want a full report."

Abby glanced at Callan's office. Day One had been the dinner with Ray and Jack. How she'd ever appeared to be so cool and confident when her insides had been bouncing around like a pinball machine, Abby would never know. Most likely her years of being onstage had helped her get through that nerve-racking night, but she'd never had a more difficult performance than that one. Callan had seemed extremely tense all through dinner, unlike his usual easygoing manner. But other than a few grumbled words, he'd hardly seemed to notice the change in her.

Day Two she'd worn a suit, but nothing like her old ones. This suit was form-fitting, in stoplight-red, and she didn't wear a blouse underneath, she wore a lace camisole that peeked over the vee of the jacket. She could have sworn she saw him stumble when he'd walked into the office, but other than that, he'd seemed completely indifferent to her.

Day Three, yesterday, hadn't fared much better. She'd worn a snug black skirt, a fitted lilac sweater and black high heels. Callan had come into the office five minutes after her, holed himself up in his office all morning and left in the afternoon without saying more than a dozen curt words. The only thing strange was the way he'd slammed the door on his way out.

Today, Day Four, she'd chosen a black, pleated skirt and beaded, moss-green cardigan sweater, but for all the attention it had got her, she might as well have worn an old bathrobe.

Sighing, Abby leaned back in her office chair. "There's nothing to report, Commander Sinclair," she said in a teasing voice. It amazed her how close she felt to Callan's sister after one whirlwind shopping trip and two days of phone calls. She'd had so few friends growing up, it felt nice to have another woman to talk to.

"He's closed his office blinds, shut his door and hasn't come out all morning."

"Hmm." There was a thoughtful pause on the line. "Are his blinds closed tight?"

Abby took off her glasses and looked closer. "I'm not sure."

"Okay, do this, then. Stick your leg out as if you've got a run in your stocking, then run your hand slowly up your leg."

Abby choked and sat up straight. "What?"

"It's a test. Just do it."

Feeling silly, Abby straightened, bent her leg as she pointed her high heel, then slid her fingertips slowly upward from the front of her calf to the hem of her pleated skirt, which she inched upward to the place where garter belt met stocking.

She jerked upright at the sound of a muffled crash inside Callan's office.

"Well?" Cara asked.

"I think I heard something," Abby whispered.

"Just my brother's eyeballs falling out of their sockets," Cara said brightly. "Or maybe his jaw hitting the floor."

He'd been watching her? She glanced at the blinds, noticed they were moving slightly, and she felt a strange tingling over her skin at the thought that he wasn't as indifferent to her as he'd been acting.

"I can't believe it," Abby said breathlessly into the phone. "How did you know?"

Cara laughed. "Like I told you, my dear. I have four big brothers, not to mention a husband. The more cool they appear on the surface, the hotter they burn underneath. And Callan, my dear, is in flames and going down."

When the outside office door opened, Abby tugged her skirt down and straightened. "Gotta go. I'll call you later."

Jack Palmer walked in holding a bouquet of yellow roses against his white polo shirt. "I was hoping I'd catch you before you went to lunch."

"Jack." Surprised, she watched his long strides close the distance between the door and her desk. "I thought you and your father were flying back to Boston this morning."

He sat on the edge of her desk and handed her the flowers. "My dad flew out. I thought I'd hang around for a couple of days."

The way he looked at her made her uncomfortable, but he'd been the perfect gentlemen with her at dinner that first night and the two times he'd called the office after that to speak to Callan. Jack had suggested dinner, just the two of them, last night, but she'd politely turned him down.

"For me?"

"I don't usually bring men flowers, so I guess so."

"Thank you." Not wanting to be rude, she took them, and once she had them, couldn't resist burying her nose in them. "But what are they for?"

"They're what I would have sent you for the wonderful time we would have had if you'd gone to dinner with me last night." He smiled. "But since you turned me down, they're a bribe to convince you to go to lunch with me today."

Abby was certain that handsome smile had knocked more than one woman's panty hose off—literally. She only wished she were one of those women. It would make her life so much easier.

But as charming as Jack Palmer was, he simply

wasn't the man she wanted. The man she thought about day and night. The man that made her burn.

But she supposed she could go to lunch with Jack. With Callan bottled up in his office, there wasn't any reason not to.

"Well, I suppose—"

Callan's office door swung open, and he walked out, his attention focused on the file folder in his hands.

"Abby, have you got the radius map on the Gibson project? I need it ASAP for—hey, Jack. What's up? I thought you went back to Boston this morning."

"Just thought I'd hang around for a couple of days, until the framing is done, if that's all right with you," Jack said easily.

"Of course, no problem. Excuse me a minute, will you?" Callan looked at Abby. "Abby, the mailing for the grading notice has to be out by three today. Can you take care of that for me?"

By three? That would take her at least three hours, and it was already noon. It wasn't reasonable that he was asking her to do that now. "I was just—"

"I'll have Reese send over some sandwiches for lunch," Callan said, then looked at Jack. "Can I get you something?"

"Some other time." Jack stood and looked at Abby. "Dinner at seven? I know a great steak house."

Good Lord, Abby thought. Suddenly both these men were trying to feed her. She felt Callan's gaze on her, but she couldn't look at him. If she did, she knew she'd tell Jack no.

"I'd love to," she said, and tried to make it sound as if she meant it.

"Great. Well, I'll get out of your way for now. See you later, Callan."

"Oh, right. See you." Callan had already turned toward his office, focused once again on the file in his
hands. He shut the door behind him.

Abby stood there for a long moment after Jack had
left and stared at Callan's closed door, certain she heard
something thud against the wall inside.

A slow smile curved her lips.

She wondered if he realized that the file he'd had
his nose buried in was upside down.

Four…five…six…

Sweating profusely, Callan sat on the end of the
bench and curled the ninety-pound barbell, struggling
to finish the last of his third set.

Seven…eight…nine…

The image of a black satin garter belt popped into
his mind. The barbell slipped from his hand, then clattered to the floor. Several heads in the gym glanced his
way. He glared at them, and they turned away.

Dammit!

He'd come straight to the gym after work, and he'd
been at it for nearly two hours. He knew he was pushing himself way beyond what his body was used to,
and that he was probably going to be sorry tomorrow,
but he'd parted company with logic and seemed to be
running with stupid at the moment.

Two hours of all-out, kick-butt pumping iron, and
he still couldn't get the damn woman out of his mind.

Gasping for breath, Callan put his hands on his knees
and leaned forward. Sweat dripped off his face, and he
reached for a towel to mop himself off.

What the hell had gotten into Abby these past few
days, anyway? he wanted to know. That tousled, just-
woke-up, sexy hairdo, the glossy pink color on her lips

that made them look wet all the time, the formfitting skirts and sweaters that showcased her killer body?

That damn garter belt.

He wiped at the fresh ring of sweat on his forehead that had nothing to do with lifting weights and everything to do with his lustful thoughts about a certain green-eyed blonde.

She wanted to keep their relationship professional and just be friends, well then, *fine*. He gritted his teeth. They could be *friends*.

He could control himself, he thought with annoyance. He hadn't touched her once this week, had he? In spite of how incredible she'd looked, he'd done everything he could to be indifferent. Damn if he hadn't wanted to, as badly as he'd wanted his next breath, but he hadn't acted on it. He had perfect control over his libido, and he intended to point that out to her when he went to her house tomorrow morning to reason with her.

Of course, she didn't need to know that he'd been sneaking an occasional peek at her. After all, he was human, for God's sake, with blood flowing in his veins. Blood that had gone from simmer to boil earlier, when she'd run those long, slender fingers of hers up those curvy, endless legs and uncovered that garter belt.

That's when his elbow had slipped off the stack of architectural books and knocked them over, which had knocked over a box of pushpins and scattered them all over his floor.

And then Mr. Jack Swift had walked in with those damn flowers and asked her to lunch. Callan had thought he'd been so clever to interfere and ask Abby to get that mailing done for him, but that had only backfired on him. Instead of lunch, which would have been quick and casual, she was now at dinner with Jack.

He tightly twisted the towel in his hands.

It was almost eight o'clock. She and pretty-boy Jack were probably sitting in a booth at the restaurant, drinking wine and laughing. The thought had his jaw tightening. Abby and alcohol were a dangerous mix. Especially the *new* Abby.

Callan knew what Jack was up to. What any man would be up to who looked at Abby. The bastard wanted to get her in bed. That was bad enough, but more, Callan was certain that Jack wanted her to come work for him and his dad.

Callan's gut twisted at the thought. He couldn't let that happen. He *had* to convince Abby to stay with him. And the only way he could do that was to convince her that he would keep their relationship strictly business.

On an oath he added another twenty pounds to the weights he'd intended to press after he'd finished his curls. Maybe three sets of eight at three hundred fifty pounds would force Abby from his mind.

He lay back flat on the bench, listened to the sound of tennis shoes slapping on treadmills and the clatter of weights dropping, the grunts and groans of the other men around him.

Yes, sir, that was what he needed to clear his thoughts and take the edge off his sexual appetite. A good, blood-pumping, heart-pounding workout.

Drawing a lungful of air, he grabbed hold of the bar over his head.

One…two…three…

Damn if that didn't feel good. He wasn't thinking about Abby at all. Or black satin garter belts.

Four…five…six…

Were her panties black satin, too? he wondered. His arms shook on count seven and eight, but he finished the set easily enough.

Breathing heavily, he waited, clenched his jaw and grabbed the bar again.

One…two…three…

And then, if her panties were black satin, her bra probably would be, too.

Four…five…six…

He ground his teeth together on a groan, imagined the feel of satin, how perfectly her soft, firm breasts fit his hands.

With another oath he dropped the bar back into its hook. His chest heaved, and the muscles in his arms burned. Dammit, anyway! He refused to let Abigail Thomas put an end to his workout.

Sucking in a deep breath, he wrapped his hands around the bar, pretended it was Jack Palmer's throat. His grip tightened.

One…two…

The edge of his vision turned white, the center blurred green. Green eyes. Deep, smoky seductive green.

"Hey, Bro, you need us to spot you?"

Lucian's voice broke through Callan's haze of pain and concentration. He blinked the sweat out of his eyes and saw Gabe standing on one side of him, Lucian the other.

Damn. They were the last thing he needed right now.

"No, dammit," he ground out between clenched teeth, and managed to heave the bar up again on the count of four.

"You sure?" Gabe asked. "You look a little shaky, there."

"I said no, didn't I?" He grunted each word loudly.

"We'll just watch, then, since you don't want our help," Lucian said with good humor, and both his brothers stood back, arms folded.

Five...I can do this...six...

No. He couldn't.

The bar came down on his chest, all three-hundred fifty pounds, trapping him.

The ultimate embarrassment.

Gabe and Lucian stood by, grinning, while Callan struggled to breathe.

"Get this damn thing off me," he gasped.

"We don't want to butt in or anything," Lucian said, scratching his neck. "Do we, Gabe?"

"Wouldn't dream of it," Gabe returned.

"You're both going to die, you know that, don't you?" Callan said weakly.

Laughing, his brothers each took an end of the bar and lifted it back into its holder. Callan lay there, gasping for breath. He'd have to kill them later. Right now he just needed to breathe.

"Pushing yourself a little hard, aren't you?" Gabe asked. "Something tweak your pin?"

"Go to hell," Callan managed between gasps.

His brothers looked at each other and smiled.

"Abby," they both said at the same time.

He scowled at them.

"Did you see her today?" Gabe said to Lucian as if Callan were no longer there. "Man, I tell you she was *hot*."

Lucian shook his head. "Couldn't be any hotter than

yesterday. She had on this great black skirt that made her legs look—''

Callan lunged at Lucian, and they went down in a flurry of arms and legs. Gabe laughed at the two of them while they flailed around on the floor without any serious blows being struck. Several people working out nearby paused to watch and wonder what had started the Sinclair brothers up this time.

When Callan collapsed on his back, his chest heaving, Lucian dragged a hand through his hair and grinned.

''I'm gonna rip out your heart,'' Callan wheezed.

''Well now, then we'd be twins,'' Lucian baited him. ''Seeing's how Abby already ripped yours out and stomped on it.''

Callan sat up slowly, it was all he had the strength to do. ''Why couldn't I have been an only child?'' he groaned.

''And miss all this fun?'' Gabe held out a hand to Callan. Reluctantly he took it. ''Not to mention free beer.''

Feeling came back into Callan's arms as he stood, and the mention of beer perked him up. ''You buying?''

''Reese is. He told us to come find you and drag your sorry butt to the tavern. It's Friday night, there's a ball game on, and he's got a cute new waitress he wants you to meet. To take your mind off Abby. We know you had a, uh, hard week.''

Callan frowned at his brother's choice of words, knowing perfectly well what he meant by the remark. There were no secrets with the Sinclairs, he thought irritably. He thought of Cara's visit—and certainly no privacy.

Oh, why the hell not? Callan heaved a sigh. He'd shower, have a beer or two with his brothers, maybe even flirt with that waitress. Maybe more. It was just the diversion he needed to keep his mind off Abby and Jack and their "date." He didn't want to think about her inviting the Armani man back to her house. If they'd be alone there...if she was wearing that damn garter belt and Jack would try to—

"So what d'ya say?" Gabe asked. "You gonna join us?"

Callan blinked, looked at Gabe, then Lucian, thought of Reese at the tavern. Four bachelors, nowhere to be, no one to answer to. That was the life.

"Damn straight, I am," he said firmly. "Have a cold one ready for me in fifteen minutes."

Jack Palmer had offered her a job.

Abby closed her front door behind her and flipped on the living room lamp. He didn't even know that she'd quit Sinclair Construction, and he'd asked her to come work for him. And the offer he'd made her, good heavens! The salary and benefits had been more than generous. She would have to be insane to turn that kind of offer down.

She hadn't given him an answer.

He hadn't pushed, though, and when she told him she would think about it, he'd moved the conversation from business to social, talked about his travels, his interest in nineteenth-century art and his collection of antique cars. He'd been a gentleman, funny and charming and handsome and very, very smooth.

But he wasn't Callan.

It was extremely difficult to be out with one man when another one was constantly popping into your mind. All night, when she hadn't been talking about Callan, in a professional capacity, she'd been thinking about him. Sometimes those thoughts had made her cheeks turn warm and her skin hot.

Peeling off the matching jacket to her new black velvet slip-dress, she wondered why she'd even worn it tonight. She certainly hadn't been interested in impressing, or encouraging, Jack. With a sigh she folded the jacket and laid it over the back of an armchair, ran her fingers over the soft, rich fabric.

Oh, who was she kidding? Somewhere in the back of her mind, she'd been hoping that Callan would turn up at the restaurant. That he would find some excuse to be there, and he'd see her with Jack and realize that he didn't want her to be with anyone else.

What an imagination she had.

What an idiot she was.

Her last day at work was Monday. Her replacement would be there, and when five o'clock came around, Abby would leave. This time for good.

Not a minute had passed that she hadn't wanted to change her mind. To simply settle for what she could get. But how could she look at herself in the mirror if she did that? If she couldn't respect herself, Callan certainly never would, either.

He wasn't a man to settle down, especially with a woman like her. She might have changed her clothes and hair, but underneath she was still Abigail Thomas. A little boring, a little dull maybe, but that was who she was, who she'd always been. Her parents and her aunts had wanted her to be something she wasn't, and she'd tried, but she'd never been happy. She knew in her heart that even though she loved Callan, she couldn't be someone she wasn't.

Cara had meant well, and Abby had appreciated her wanting to help, but changing who she was on the outside didn't change who she was on the inside. She might not want to go back to the frumpy suits and starched blouses, but she wasn't a femme fatale, either.

Deciding that she needed a nice hot cup of tea to settle her nerves, she headed for the kitchen. Jack had suggested drinks back at his hotel, but Abby wasn't naïve enough to think that he wanted to talk about her coming to work for his father's company, so she'd turned him down. If she went to work for the Palmers, she would have to make Jack understand that she was only interested in the job, not him.

She'd already made that mistake and had no intention of ever taking that road again. She was also determined not to sit around and feel sorry for herself for the rest of the evening. Determined not to think about Callan every minute, every second. To wonder what he'd done tonight. If he'd given her a second thought. Or even a first thought.

She was halfway to the kitchen when she heard the quiet knock at her front door. She prayed that it wasn't Jack. Even though she'd met him at the restaurant, her address and phone number were listed, and she would be easy to find if he thought that he might want to try to change her mind about the job…or anything else.

But if it wasn't Jack…

Her heart pounding, she glanced through her peephole and saw Callan standing in the yellow glow of her porch light.

He knocked again. Louder.

Don't answer it, said the voice of reason.

Breath held, she touched the door.

Just say hello, her heart said.

She spread her palm on the door.

Invite him in, her body screamed.

The door vibrated with his next heavy knock, and she jerked her hand away.

"Abby, dammit, are you in there?" he called out.

Well, that certainly was curt, she thought. If he'd come here to yell or fuss at her, or be a bully, then he could just leave. And she'd tell him so right to his face.

Straightening her shoulders, she opened the door.

He opened his mouth to say something, but then he simply stood there, mute, and stared at her. When his gaze turned dark and hot, then scorched her from head to toe, she realized how little her dress covered.

"Callan." She felt her knees weaken at the fierce expression on his face. To keep her legs from buckling under her, she held on tightly to the doorknob with one hand and the doorjamb with the other. "Is something wrong?"

"Yes, dammit," he said tightly. "Something sure as hell is wrong."

And then he moved so quickly, grabbed her and had his mouth on hers with such lightning speed that all she could do was hold on.

Eleven

This was definitely not what he'd intended.

He'd just wanted to talk to her, he'd told himself all the way here from the tavern. Reason with her. Discuss the situation logically.

See if Jack Palmer had come back to her place.

So when she'd opened the door, when he'd realized that Jack wasn't there, he'd taken one look at her and just lost it.

Now here he stood, practically devouring her.

Shocked by his own lack of control, Callan yanked his mouth from Abby's and stared down at her. Her cheeks were flushed, her lips still moist from his kiss. All week long she'd driven him crazy with her new style, her perfume, her hair, her clothes. But tonight, good God, tonight she absolutely destroyed him.

The slim velvet dress she wore screamed, ''Take me,'' and her hair, gathered up on top of her head in a fountain of curls, begged to be loosened so it could tumble around her smooth, ivory shoulders. And her scent, the same scent that had invaded his senses, his very soul, for the past four days, now drew him to her like a bear to honey.

He tightened his hands on her shoulders, clenched his jaw so tightly he'd probably have to see a dentist for a cracked tooth.

When her lashes fluttered open, he saw a mixture of surprise and desire and confusion in the deep-dark-green of her eyes.

God, she tasted sweet. Smooth and silky, with a subtle hint of mint and chocolate that reminded him of the wrapped candy restaurants sometimes gave with the checks. Abby was like one of those candies, he thought dimly, and he wanted desperately to unwrap and taste her again.

With a will of iron, he slowly loosened his fierce hold on her and stepped away. "I'm sorry," he said tightly, though he wasn't certain he meant it. "I swear to you, I didn't come here to do that."

Touching her lips, she drew in a slow, shaky breath. "Am I supposed to be relieved by that or disappointed?"

He frowned at her. "Dammit, Abby, I said I was sorry. What more do you want from me?"

"I don't want anything from you, Callan," she said coolly. "If you recall, you came here, pounded on my door and then grabbed me."

Of course he did, like some kind of maniac, he thought. What the hell was the matter with him? He'd come here to talk to her, not argue. And certainly not to kiss her.

Cursing himself, he dragged a hand through his hair

and let out a long breath. "I'm sorry," he said again, this time without the edge of anger or need. "I just came here to talk to you, and then you opened the door…"

…looking like a goddess, and all I could think was "Mine…"

She tilted her head, waited for him to continue.

"…and I just sort of forgot myself," he finished, carefully keeping his attention on her face. He didn't dare look anywhere else or, God help him, he'd probably grab her again.

"I promise not to do that again," he said with tremendous effort. "But I'll leave if you want me to."

He felt his heart drop when she moved toward the door, but when she closed it and turned back around to face him, he felt as if he had a hammer swinging in his chest.

"I was going to make some herbal tea. Would you like some?"

"Sure." He would drink radiator fluid as long as she let him stay. He followed her to the kitchen, only letting his gaze drop to the sway of her hips once before yanking it back up again. If he could just keep his eyes on her face and his mind on business, then he could do this.

He could, dammit.

He stared at a picture of a flower-filled wheelbarrow on the wall, realized that it was the same kind of fine-point, needle-and-yarn work that he'd seen his sister do. With fingers as slender and graceful as Abby had, he wasn't surprised at her skill with a needle. But when his thoughts wandered to how those fingers had touched him, *where* she'd touched him and what she could do to him, his throat went dry, and he forced his attention elsewhere.

And saw the vase of red roses on the counter.

While she filled a kettle with water, he eased his way over and glanced at the card. "Thinking of you."

Dammit. They had to be from Jack. And from the look of the flowers, he'd sent them a couple of days ago, before that bouquet he'd brought today. Damn smooth son-of-a-gun.

I should have sent flowers, he thought. Hell, he would have sent over a damn truckload if he'd thought it would help his case. But how could it? If he'd sent flowers, she would think he was putting the move on her, which was exactly the reason she was leaving.

He didn't know what the hell to do, and it was driving him nuts. She was driving him nuts.

She flipped on the gas burner, and the blue flame leaped under the kettle. When she turned around, she folded her arms and leveled her gaze with his. "What did you want to talk about?"

He could hardly say that he'd come over to tell her that they could work together, that they *could* have a professional relationship that was strictly business. After that kiss, he'd pretty well destroyed that strategy. He would simply have to find a new tactic to keep her from leaving Sinclair Construction. As soon as he figured one out, he'd do just that.

So he had to talk to her about something. Had to have some reason he'd come over here. He stared at the flowers again. "Jack Palmer."

"Jack?" She narrowed her gaze. "What about him?"

"Did he offer you a job?" *Did he try to get you in bed?*

"As a matter of fact, he did."

Callan felt a muscle jump in his jaw, tried to remember which question he'd voiced out loud and which one he'd thought. "What did you say?"

"I haven't given him an answer."

The knot in his gut eased a bit. *Thank God.* "Abby—"

"I'm not staying at Sinclair Construction, either. Monday is my last day. Mrs. Green, the woman replacing me, is a widow whose husband owned a large construction company in Philadelphia. She ran the company for thirty years. She'll be perfect for the job."

You're perfect, he wanted to say, but could see that stubborn tilt to her chin and knew it would get him nowhere.

He started to turn, thinking it best to leave before he made matters worse, but then he stopped.

What the hell. If she'd absolutely made up her mind not to come back, then how could he make matters worse?

He spun back around. "Listen to me, and listen carefully." He watched her eyes widen as he moved slowly toward her. "I want *you.*"

How those words thrilled Abby. And excited. There was a sharp, primal glint in his eyes, and when he reached out and touched her face, her heart skipped, then started to race.

"I don't want anybody else," Callan said, his voice quiet and strained. "Not just in the office, but all the time. And right now, at this moment, I want you so bad it hurts."

Torn between leaning into him or stepping away, she held still, breath held, and waited. Waited for him to say how much he cared for *her,* not just in bed, and

not just the Abby with a new hairstyle wearing sexy
clothes, but the real Abigail Thomas.

Only she wasn't even sure who that was anymore.
Somewhere the line between who she had been before
they made love and who she was now had become
fuzzy.

But the words she wanted, that she needed, didn't
come, and standing here with the man she loved so
deeply, hearing him say he wanted her, every good
drop of sense she had flew out the window, every bit
of logic and reason vanished like smoke. She'd told
herself she wouldn't settle for less than love, but for
this moment only, she knew she would.

She understood what he meant when he said he
wanted her so badly it hurt. She hurt, too. Physically,
yes, she ached for him to touch her, to kiss her. But it
was her heart that hurt the most.

"Abby, for God's sake," he said hoarsely. "Talk to
me."

*Talk about how much I love you, then watch you run
for the hills?* she thought. Or worse, he might laugh at
her. Or the worst of all, feel pity. She couldn't do it,
couldn't survive the pain. She wanted only good memories, only the ones she could take with her and hold
close.

Without taking her eyes from his, she reached behind
her and turned off the burner on the stove and lifted
her face to his.

"Kiss me."

He went still, then his arms were around her, lifting
her. Melting into him, she slid her hands up his chest,
around his neck. Heat shot through her veins, went
from simmer to boil; her heart swelled and pounded.
Glorious, she thought. *Marvelous.*

Good heavens. She was ready to break into song.

But when he suddenly spun her, lifted her onto the counter, her mind went blank. She felt the cupboards on her back, the cool tile under her thighs and his mouth consuming her with an urgency, an intensity, that made her head spin.

A low, soft moan rose from the depths of her throat. His wonderful, sensual assault on her mouth continued, and she met each hot, wet thrust of his tongue, trembled when he slid her to the edge of the counter and pushed her dress up.

He moaned loudly.

"Abby," he said raggedly, breaking the kiss to stare down at her garter belt. His fingers slid over black satin, and she trembled. "Tell me you know CPR, or I'm a dead man."

Laughing softly, she watched him move his hands over the soft, sensitive flesh of her inner thighs. Trembling, she closed her eyes and leaned back. He inched her dress up higher and parted her legs, stepping between them and intimately closing the distance between their bodies. She felt rough denim and hard male press against the vee of her thighs. She wrapped her legs around him, drawing him closer.

His scent, soap and man and sex, excited her, aroused her as surely as his hands which were now sliding the straps of her dress off her shoulders, easing velvet down. He filled his hands with her, kneaded, caressed, then bent to taste.

On a moan, she let her head fall back when he managed the hook of her strapless bra and tossed the strip of black satin behind her. His warm breath skimmed over her skin and when he took one beaded nipple in his mouth, she arched upward and dragged her hands through his hair. He was the one killing her, she thought, and cried out when his tongue swirled hotly over her. Shimmering waves of desire coursed through her blood and pooled between her legs.

"Callan," she whispered, reached for the buckle on his belt, nimbly worked it free. "Make love to me. Now."

Abby's words inflamed Callan, snapped the last thread of his control. He'd never experienced anything like this before, never felt so completely off balance. He couldn't get a foothold on what was happening here, but when she flipped open the snap of his jeans, he absolutely couldn't think, he could only feel.

Her skin, milky-white against the black satin of her underwear, was smooth and soft. He slid his hands over her flat stomach, her hips; his fingertips lingered for a moment on the straps of her garter belt, then slipped deeper and touched warm, quivering skin, slipped deeper still into the damp heat of her. Sweat beaded his forehead. He caught her mouth again as he stroked, brought her to the edge. Her soft moans and the sensual rocking of her hips brought him to the edge, as well, and he knew he had to have her now.

Her panties were nothing more than a thin strip across her hips, and he hooked one finger underneath and yanked. She gasped, and when he brought her to him and drove himself inside of her, she made a soft, wild sound deep in her throat that made his blood boil.

She hung on, met every hard, deep thrust, until her body tightened fiercely around him and she cried out, shuddering against him, into him. He felt the bite of her nails through his shirt, plunged deeper into her as his own shattering climax slammed into him. The sound he made was primitive, victorious, and he buried his face into her neck, wishing desperately that he could pull her inside of him.

Several long moments passed before he could breathe, then several more before he could speak. As the insanity eased, he realized that they were still in the kitchen. Good Lord. The kitchen.

"Abby," he said, his voice strained, "I...I'm sorry. I should have at least made it to the bedroom."

When he started to ease away, she held him tightly to her. "We will," she murmured, then kissed his neck, his shoulder.

He laughed softly, wrapped his arms around her as he carried her to the bedroom. Abigail Thomas was one amazing woman.

And from out of nowhere Cara's words echoed in his head, *Watch out for cliffs,* and he was suddenly afraid, terrified that he finally understood what she had meant.

He woke to the sound of an early-morning summer rain and Abby murmuring in her sleep beside him. She had one lovely, long, smooth leg draped over his and her cheek on his chest. Her tousled hair lay like a golden silk scarf across his shoulder. He couldn't remember ever feeling this contented.

Or satisfied.

Gently he brushed a strand of hair from her eyes, tempted to give in to the urge to wake her just so he could kiss those amazing lips of hers. But since he'd kept her up most of the night, or she'd kept him up— he grinned—he thought it best to let her sleep a little longer.

Although, maybe not too much longer, he decided

as her fingers moved restlessly, even though she was still asleep.

Surely she would listen to reason now, he thought, covering her hand with his. They were great together, in bed and out. They could date each other and still work together. People did it all the time. Who the hell cared what those damn magazines said?

This wasn't a *fling*. This was…well, this was a relationship. An exclusive one. She wouldn't see anyone else, and neither would he.

He smiled at the idea, suddenly felt ravenous. When she murmured something again, he pressed his lips to her forehead.

"Abby," he said softly.

"Hmm." Her warm breath fanned his chest.

"I'd love a great big breakfast," he teased.

"I love you, too," she murmured back, and snuggled her head in the crook of his arm.

His smile faded. He went very, very still. Struggled to breathe.

Whoa. Hit the pause button.

Love?

She loved him?

Abby isn't the type to take love lightly. That's what Cara had said, Callan remembered. He felt the blood drain from his head. To a woman love meant marriage, which meant house and kids and dog and mortgage. The word *husband* popped into his mind, and he felt his skin turn cold.

When the phone beside the bed rang, he started to reach for it, but Abby jerked awake and grabbed it instead.

"Hello."

Damn, but she sounded sexy in the morning, her

voice deep and husky and laced with sleep. When she sat on the edge of the bed, she also offered a spectacular view of her bare back. He propped his head in his hand and followed the curve of her shoulders down to her hips.

"Oh, good morning." That glorious back of hers straightened, and she glanced over her shoulder at him. "No, it's not too early."

Callan frowned. He thought nine o'clock on a Saturday was early. Who the hell was she talking to?

His jaw tightened when she laughed softly. Jack Palmer, dammit. Callan knew it was him.

Business client or not, Callan decided he'd rip the guy apart.

"I'd like to get back to you on that. Yes, I do have your number." She paused. "All right. Yes, I will."

When she hung up and started to reach for her robe, he snagged her arm and dragged her back into bed with him. She tumbled against him, her eyes still sleepy, her lips rosy and still swollen from his kisses last night.

"That was Jack Palmer, wasn't it?" he said more roughly than he intended. "What the hell is he calling you at home for?"

"Callan—"

"You're not taking that job, dammit."

Abby sighed, then combed her fingers through her hair. "That's my decision. One I haven't made yet."

"You like it here in Bloomfield. You told me that. Why would you leave?"

"Monday is my last day at work." She kept her gaze level with his. "I'm considering all other options."

"Well, consider this," he said tightly. "Jack just wants to get you in bed."

Her green eyes frosted over. "Well, if that were true,

then I suppose my life wouldn't be any different in Boston than it is here, would it?''

"Don't you dare compare me with Jack Palmer." Callan felt his blood go on fast boil. "It's not like that with you and me.''

"And what is it like, then?'' she asked evenly.

What was it like? He opened his mouth, closed it again. Hell, he didn't know.

Her words, *I love you, too,* felt like a weight settling on his chest, making it hard to breathe. He heard the rain falling heavier now.

"It's just different." He swung out of bed and grabbed his jeans. "I have to go to the job site and cover up lumber. We'll talk about this later.''

He wanted desperately to grab her to him, to say something, *anything,* but he was too tied up in knots, and he was certain he'd said too much already. When he calmed down later, he'd be able to talk to her in a more rational manner, make her see it was ridiculous for her to leave Bloomfield. Right now he just wanted to yell.

She said nothing as she watched him dress—or when he snatched her to him and fiercely kissed her goodbye.

She said nothing except goodbye.

Abby stared out her kitchen window, watched the drops gather on the glass, then slide slowly down the panes. The sound of water dripping off the eaves of her roof mixed with the sputter of coffee brewing in the pot.

She hated that Callan had left angry, especially after the wonderful night they'd shared, but she wasn't surprised. Because they'd made love last night, she was certain he thought that she'd changed her mind about leaving, that everything would be fine again. He'd never taken her seriously, any more than he'd taken their making love seriously. He no doubt assumed that whenever the urge struck, they would jump into bed again.

She'd asked him right to his face how *his* wanting to sleep with her or Jack Palmer wanting to sleep with her was different, and he hadn't been able to give her an answer. Which was an answer in itself.

She knew without a doubt that she and Callan could never work together again, that they could never just be friends, as she'd suggested before. She loved him too much for that. Every time she saw him, her heart would tear open again. How could she move on, get on with her life, knowing that she might turn around in the market or the post office and he'd be there? That when he didn't want her anymore, he would be with other women. What would she do if she saw him with someone else, smiling at another woman, holding her hand or even kissing her?

The thought ripped through her like a dull knife. She couldn't live with that. He'd made it clear he wasn't the marrying type, and sex, as wonderful as it was, wasn't enough for her.

All or nothing, she thought, and sat at the kitchen table. The open Yellow Pages advertisements stared back at her.

Sabrini Brothers. Expert Movers. Short Notice Welcome.

Abby made a note of the number. She wondered if today was too short notice and glanced at the next ad.

Westworld Movers. We Move Memories. Insured Against Breakage.

We move memories. Abby felt the moisture burn her

eyes as she wrote that number down on her list, wishing the breakage insurance included hearts.

At the sound of the doorbell, the heart in question slammed in her chest. Callan wouldn't be back this soon. She didn't want him to be, couldn't stand to face him right now. She knew she would say the one thing he wouldn't want to hear. *I love you.*

Her hand shook as she opened the door. It wasn't Callan.

"Hello, sweetheart," Aunt Ruby and Aunt Emerald said together.

Wide-eyed, she stared at her aunts.

"May we come in, dear?" Ruby asked when Abby didn't say anything. "It's a bit wet out here."

Abby blinked, then threw the door open and stepped aside. "Oh, I'm sorry. Of course."

That's when she noticed the cane Emerald was using and the look of pain on her face as she limped into the house. "Aunt Emerald, what happened?"

Emerald shook her head, winced with every step as she moved to the sofa. "Such a silly thing. Ruby and I were visiting the Rhumba Club in Miami. I missed a tango step and ended up with a twisted ankle."

"But your cruise." Abby looked at the thick layers of bandage wrapped around Emerald's ankle. "You're supposed to leave tomorrow."

"Such is life." Ruby sighed and sat down beside Emerald. "I'm afraid we won't be going anywhere for a while. We thought we'd visit with you and Callan for a few more days before we head back to New York. Is he home, dear?"

Abby looked at her aunts, saw the bright, expectant

look in their eyes. She couldn't lie to them anymore. She was done pretending.

Straightening her shoulders, she sank into the armchair and faced them. "Aunt Emerald, Aunt Ruby, there's something I have to tell you."

Twelve

The weather seemed to mirror Callan's mood. Dark, heavy and just muggy enough to bring out a sweat. He'd spent the morning covering equipment and tools, and with the last tarp finally in place, he stomped up the trailer's steps behind Lucian, scrubbed the worst of the mud off his boots, then stepped inside.

"Damn rain." He stalked over to the coffeepot, poured a cup, nearly choked on the pungent fumes. "God, Lucian, if the toxic-waste inspector comes by, you're in for one hell of a fine."

He took a sip, anyway, then swore fluently when he burned his tongue.

"You're looking a little ragged around the edges today, Cal." Lucian grabbed a cup of coffee himself, then settled back in his chair. "Something gnawing on you?"

"Just your mouth," Callan grumbled.

Lucian grinned. "Maybe that sweet mood of yours has something to do with where you went after you left the tavern early last night."

"Who said I went anywhere?"

"So, did she slam the door in your face?"

"Shut the hell up." Without thinking, he took another sip of the sludge in his cup, wincing when he burned his tongue again.

Lucian's grin widened. "I've got a choice for you, Cal. Either we can go a couple of rounds, and I'll knock off that chip you've got on your shoulder, or you can tell your little brother all about it."

"Here's a choice for you," he snapped back. "Either you can shut up or kiss my—"

"Damn, it's starting to come down hard," Gabe said as he walked in, slapped his black cowboy hat against his leg then settled it back on his head. "Hi, kids."

"Hey, Gabe, pull up a chair." Lucian folded his hands behind his head. "Your little brother here was about to tell me all about his love life."

Gabe headed for the coffeepot. "That shouldn't take longer than thirty seconds."

"Who the hell said anything about love?" Callan swiped a hand over his face. "Did I say anything about love?"

I love you, too.

He couldn't get the words, or the woman who'd whispered them, out of his mind.

Brows raised, Gabe looked at Lucian. "He really does have it bad."

"Appears that way."

"The hell I do," Callan barked. "She's just a woman, a damn complicated one at that, and do I need complications? Hell, no. Light and easy, that's my motto. Keeps everything simple.''

"Yeah, simple.'' Gabe raised his cup to Callan. "That sounds like you.''

"You're supposed to be on my side, dammit.'' Callan slammed his coffee cup on the desk and stood. Then started to pace. He sure as hell wasn't going to tell them that Abby had told him she loved him. "Palmer offered her a job.''

Gabe whistled softly. "Did she take it?''

"She's *considering* it.'' He raked both hands through his hair. "If she loves me, dammit, why the hell would she be *considering* it?''

Callan froze, clamped his mouth shut, though obviously too late. Dammit anyway, why had he blurted *that* out?

"So, she told you that, did she?'' Gabe lifted one brow.

"No wonder he's in such a mood today,'' Lucian said, sucking his cheeks in. "Looks like our boy's bit the big one.''

"I haven't 'bit' a damn thing.''

"Why don't you put yourself out of misery and marry the girl?'' Lucian said with good humor. "Course, that would be putting Abby in misery, but she'd have three understanding brothers-in-law and one sister-in-law to ease her pain.''

"Marry?'' Callan choked on the word. "Why the hell would I get married?''

"That's true.'' Gabe took a sip of coffee and grimaced. "There's all those other women out there waiting for you. By the way, that cute little waitress at the tavern asked me for your phone number.''

He wasn't one bit interested in that waitress. The only woman he thought about was Abby.

The only woman he wanted was Abby.

"And now that Abby's come out of her shell, you might say," Lucian said, picking up where Gabe had left off, "she probably wants to have a little variety herself. I doubt she wants to marry anybody, especially old sweet-tempered Cal here, until she looks around a bit more. Too bad she's not hanging around Bloomfield. Maybe she'd like to look my way. I'm prettier than Cal, anyway."

They were trying to make him mad, Callan knew. Trying to get a rise out of him. And it was working, dammit. Red swam in front of his eyes, and he clenched his fists at his sides.

The phone rang, and Lucian picked it up, then grinned at Callan.

Abby, Callan thought, and though his pulse did jump, he felt a certain smug satisfaction that she would call so soon. In the entire year that he'd known her, they'd never had any kind of argument before. She'd probably been crying all morning and was finally ready to talk reason.

He took the phone and with his brothers watching, said casually into the phone, "Yeah?"

It wasn't Abby.

"We're sorry to bother you, dear." Aunt Emerald sat on Abby's sofa, her leg propped up comfortably on top of a pillow on the coffee table. "But after Abby explained everything, how you'd pretended to be engaged so we wouldn't be so concerned about her, well, we just felt that we should apologize to you in person for putting you through all that nonsense. If she had just said something to us, we could have saved you both so much trouble.''

It had taken Callan less than twenty minutes to get back to Abby's house from the site after Ruby's phone call. Bubbling with energy and dressed in a loose-fitting fluorescent-orange pantsuit, she'd met him at the door and led him in, then flounced off to the kitchen to make him a cup of tea.

He glanced toward the door leading to the bedrooms, wondered if Abby was back there. After the way he'd left this morning, well, maybe he could understand that she might not want to see him for a while. He just needed to get her alone, talk with her.

It was all he could do to listen to Emerald speaking to him, but he forced his attention back to her.

''Abby must be very special to you.'' Emerald had both hands on the top of her cane. ''On a professional level, I mean. For you to go to such lengths to keep her in your office, well, she must be extremely proficient.''

''Ah, well, yes, she is very…special.'' He looked at the hall doorway again. Dammit, why wouldn't she come out?

''I have to tell you,'' Ruby said as she came back into the room with a steaming mug in her hands, ''you certainly had us fooled. Heavens, just looking at you and Abby together, I was absolutely convinced you two were deeply in love. You can imagine Emerald's and my surprise to learn you and Abby don't have any romantic affection for each other at all.''

But he *did* have affection for Abby. Tremendous affection. And of course it was romantic, he thought, though the realization made a knot form in his throat.

He glanced toward the bedrooms again. He *had* to see her.

He jerked his gaze back to Ruby. "Ah, could you ask Abby if it would be all right if I came back and spoke with her a minute?"

"Abby?" Ruby wrinkled her forehead. "Abby's not here."

"She's not here?"

Ruby and Emerald glanced at each other, then looked dolefully at him. "Oh, dear." Ruby touched her hand to her chest. "We assumed she called you while she was packing her suitcase."

"Suitcase?" Callan felt the knot in his throat tighten. "Why was she packing her suitcase?"

"Well, since Emerald and I couldn't go on our cruise, we gave Abby one of our tickets. We thought a getaway to the Caribbean would be good for her before she moved to Boston."

Moved? To Boston? His heart slammed against his ribs. *Caribbean cruise?* How could she leave without telling him? Without even speaking to him first? She was supposed to be in love with him, dammit!

He drew in a slow, deep breath to keep himself from yelling. It felt as if his skull had shrunk and was pressing in on his brain. He opened his mouth, but his throat had closed up.

She *couldn't* leave, he thought wildly. He wouldn't let her. He wanted her here, with him, he needed her, he…

Oh, God. He loved her.

"Are you all right, dear?" Ruby asked. "You look a little pale."

He'd never felt this way before. He didn't know

what to do about it. What to do *with* it. Too weak to stand, he sank back down on the chair.

"Fine," he mumbled. "I'm fine."

He loved her. He wanted to be with her. Only her. He wanted that damn house and dog and mortgage. Little Sinclairs.

His throat went dry.

He realized that he'd expected her to stay, to work for him, to be with him, but he hadn't offered her what she'd really wanted, what she needed. He'd expected her to settle for good enough, just as she'd done her entire life. Abby deserved more than good enough.

And now she was gone.

Dammit, she'd told him that she loved him. *I love you, too.* That's what she'd said.

But she hadn't even been awake. What if she hadn't meant it? What if she'd just been murmuring in her sleep? What if she really didn't love him, now that he'd realized that he was in love with her?

"She did leave a letter." Ruby reached for an envelope on the coffee table and handed it to him. "I was supposed to deliver it on Monday morning, but since you're here, I don't see any reason not to give it to you now."

Callan didn't even care that he nearly ripped the envelope to shreds in order to get it open, then yanked out the letter inside.

And instantly became a speed reader.

Dear Callan,
Once again I apologize to you for leaving so suddenly. As I told you before, I have enjoyed my past year at Sinclair Construction. Thank you for allowing me the opportunity to work for you.

On a personal level, I want you to know how much I appreciate what you did in order to help me out of the foolish situation I placed myself in. I have explained everything to Aunt Emerald and Aunt Ruby, and they were remarkably understanding, even amused. I'm sure that one day both you and I will also laugh when we look back on this time.

Callan ground his teeth together. Laugh? Like hell he would.

Mrs. Green will be an extremely competent replacement for me and addition to Sinclair Construction. I am sorry I will not be there Monday on her first day of work, but with her experience, she needs no training or instruction. I am confident you will be very satisfied with her performance.

Since my aunts will be having my things sent to Boston while I'm away, I do not expect we will see each other again. But please know that I will always remember you fondly.

Abigail

She would remember him *fondly?*

He sat there, frozen in his chair, with the crumpled edges of the letter between his stiff, cold fingers.

Emerald leaned forward on her cane. "Is something wrong, Callan?"

He blinked, then glanced up. "When did she leave?" he asked tightly.

"Oh, dear, well, let's see." Emerald stared at her thin gold wristwatch for what felt like hours, muttering and counting to herself. "She left the house maybe two hours ago, but her plane to Miami leaves in ten minutes.''

Ten minutes! Dammit! He'd never make it to the airport to stop her. "How can I get in touch with her?''

Ruby and Emerald looked at each other, then Ruby shook her head. "I'm afraid you can't. We don't even know where she's staying tonight, and the ship leaves tomorrow morning.''

He was out of his chair like a rocket, dragging a hand through his hair. "What time?''

"I have that information right here on the ticket we're not using.'' Ruby picked up the travel packet sitting on the coffee table and started to fumble through it. "I suppose we should have just turned this ticket in, or at least called the cruise company, but we do have cancellation insurance. Now where is that itinerary?''

"May I?'' His hands itched to snatch the packet from her hands.

"Oh, yes, of course.'' Ruby handed him the thick envelope. "In fact, why don't you just take it? There might be something in there that can help you. You can bring it back later, when you're done. Would you like a warm-up on your tea, dear?''

"No, thank you. I have to go.'' He was already heading for the door when he turned abruptly. "Don't move anything of Abby's,'' he said roughly. "Not one thing.''

Brows raised, they both looked at him. "But, Callan—''

"Not one blessed thing. Promise.''

"Well,'' Emerald said hesitantly. "I suppose a couple of days wouldn't really matter.''

He stalked back into the room, kissed a startled Emerald and Ruby on the cheek, then flew out of the house.

Emerald and Ruby stared at the closed door for one long, quiet minute, then Ruby rose and moved into the kitchen. Humming softly, she returned to the living room with a bottle of champagne that she and Emerald had brought back from Miami.

Ruby opened the champagne and poured two glasses.

The Miami air was warm and balmy, the sky deep-blue. A breeze whispered through the open bedroom cabin window, carrying with it the scent of salt and ocean water. The sound of reggae music and people laughing drifted up from the deck below.

They'd set sail only moments before, and the cruise liner swayed lightly as they made their way out of port. The ship was beautiful, Abby thought. Huge, sleek and shiny with polished brass and gleaming woods. She'd been lost in a maze of hallways and staircases after she'd managed to wade through luggage and ticket check-in, and now, standing here in the luxurious suite her aunts had reserved, she felt more lost than ever.

She still wasn't sure what she was doing here. One minute she'd been apologizing to them for lying about her engagement to Callan, told them that she was con-sidering moving to Boston, and the next minute they were stuffing clothes into a suitcase for her and shoving her out the door to a waiting taxi.

Aunt Emerald had insisted that if she and Ruby couldn't go, then their own precious niece and dear sister's daughter most certainly would. If she hadn't been in such a muddled state of mind, Abby knew she would have dug her heels in and stayed home.

But the more she'd thought about it, the more the idea had appealed to her. Maybe she did need to get away, have a little fun. Stop thinking about Callan every second.

She didn't want to remember him the way he'd left her yesterday morning, angry and cold and distant. She only wanted to remember his all-consuming smile, the sound of his deep laugh, the way he narrowed his dark eyes when he was deep in thought. Just thinking about the texture of his large, rough hands on her skin, the press of his mouth on her lips, his strong, muscled body moving over hers made her tingle all the way down to her toes. No one had ever made her feel like that before. She was certain no one ever would again.

She glanced at the king-size bed, the bucket of champagne and basket of fruit that the travel agent had sent, and she was certain she could feel her heart shattering into even tinier pieces than it already had.

Well, enough of feeling sorry for herself, she decided. She'd have a good time if it killed her. She intended to mingle and dance and even have one of those Bahama mama drinks that the waiters carried around on trays. Maybe she'd even have two.

A man's voice came over the ship's speaker system advising everyone to put on their life jackets for a drill on the outside decks. She found the bright-orange jacket inside a closet and slipped the bulky vest over the pale-yellow sundress she had on, then stared at herself in the full-length mirror on the outside of the closet. Laughing at how silly she looked, she started to turn away, then slowly turned back and stared at herself.

This was the new Abigail Thomas, she thought, and squared her shoulders, hardly recognizing the woman staring back at her with startled green eyes and flushed cheeks. No more hiding behind those frumpy suits and spinster hairstyles, no more waiting around for something to happen to her. The new Abby *made* things happen. She was a mover and a shaker. A confident, secure woman who knew what she wanted and went after it.

As much as she loved him, as much as it hurt, she would have to learn to live without Callan Sinclair. It would be the hardest thing she would ever have to do, but she would. She would survive, and though it was hard to believe at the moment, she was certain she would be stronger.

Outside she could hear the porters knocking on doors, checking cabins and instructing passengers which deck to go to for the safety drill. No exceptions, all passengers must attend.

When the knock came at her own cabin, she sighed, then opened the door.

And thought she was hallucinating.

Wearing a bright-blue Hawaiian-print shirt and faded blue jeans, Callan filled the doorway. Sunglasses dangled from his shirt pocket.

"I'm here for the lifesaving drill," he said calmly, then stepped into the cabin and closed the door behind him.

She couldn't speak, couldn't breathe. And when he dragged her into his arms and kissed her, she couldn't even think.

His mouth was hard against hers, demanding, and she felt her bones melt with the kiss. Before the last thread of reason snapped, she pressed her palms against his chest and yanked her lips from his.

"What are you doing here?" she gasped. "*How* did you get here?"

"It wasn't easy. The first flight I could catch out of Philadelphia barely made it here in time, then I had to give the taxi driver an extra hundred to get me here before the ship sailed."

He *was* real, she realized, feeling the strong ripple of muscle under her palms, the hard, rapid beat of his heart. "I don't understand."

"All I is can say is that your aunts' travel agent is a miracle worker. She has all our business from now own."

Our business? She shook her head, trying to clear the fog that seemed to have settled in her brain. "Callan, what are you talking about?"

"You're not moving to Boston."

"I'm not?"

"You're not. You're staying in Bloomfield. With me."

She was glad he was still holding her because her legs had turned to the consistency of warm rubber. His hands tightened on her shoulders, and she watched him swallow hard.

"I love you," he said firmly, then more gently, "I love you, Abby."

She blinked, certain she'd heard him wrong. "You…love…me?"

He nodded. "And I know you love me, too. You told me."

"I told you I loved you?"

"I don't care if you were half-asleep when you said it, the fact is you did say it, and I'm holding you to it."

Her eyes widened. She'd told him that she loved him

in her sleep? And what did he mean, he was holding her to it?

"Callan—"

"We're getting married. We can do it here, on the ship, or when we get back. Whatever you want, as long as you say yes."

Married? He wanted to *marry* her?

When he reached into his pocket and pulled out the engagement ring she'd returned, then slipped it on her finger, she felt the moisture gather in her eyes. She was glad she had a life preserver on because she suddenly felt as if she were drowning.

Overcome by the swell of emotions inside her, all Abby could do was stare at the ring. She *was* hallucinating. She had some strange kind of cruise-ship fever. What else could explain what was happening?

When she didn't answer right away, Callan's eyes narrowed with determination. "For the past year you've been a quiet, calming breeze in my life that I'd counted on, but taken for granted. Then suddenly you were gone and there was a tornado where that breeze had been. I've been crazy ever since. Crazy about you, Abby. Crazy about the way your forehead furrows when you're typing and the way your glasses slip down that cute little nose of yours. I love how your cheeks turn rosy-pink when you blush and your chin goes up a notch when you set your mind to something. I'm even crazy about Stanley, that silly bird you give peanuts to."

Stanley? He liked Stanley? Heavens, he does look a little crazed, Abby thought, and nearly laughed with the wonder of it all.

He pulled her closer to him. "It's not just sex, Abby, but I'd be a liar to tell you that making love with you isn't the most incredible, the most amazing thing that has ever happened to me. I love you, dammit. Everything about you. Even that silly vest you're wearing.''

Her laugh was cut short when he dragged her into his arms and kissed her again. She leaned into him, her mind spinning, then suddenly he yanked his mouth from hers.

"Say you love me," he insisted. "That you'll marry me.''

"I love you.'' Breathless, she touched his cheeks with her hands. "I'll marry you.''

He hugged her fiercely, lifted her off the ground and spun her while his mouth covered hers. "Take this thing off,'' he rasped, pulling at the ties on her vest.

"There's a lifesaving drill,'' she murmured against his lips. "We have to go.''

"You've already saved my life, Abby. Don't you know that?'' He backed her toward the bedroom.

Laughing, she wrapped her arms around his neck. "Do you have the feeling that Aunt Emerald and Aunt Ruby orchestrated this?''

"No question about it.'' He closed the bedroom door and locked it. "We definitely have to remember to thank them when we get back.''

"Oh, yes,'' she whispered, and sucked in a breath as he lowered her to the bed. "Yes, yes, yes.''

*   *   *   *   *

*Don't miss Gabe's story,
coming in August from
Silhouette Intimate Moments.*

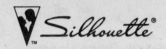
Silhouette®

where love comes alive—online...

Visit the *Author's Alcove*

➤ Find the most complete information anywhere on your favorite Silhouette author.

➤ Try your hand in the Writing Round Robin— contribute a chapter to an online book in the making.

Enter the *Reading Room*

➤ Experience an interactive novel—help determine the fate of a story being created now by one of your favorite authors.

➤ Join one of our reading groups and discuss your favorite book.

Drop into *Shop eHarlequin*

➤ Find the latest releases—read an excerpt or write a review for this month's Silhouette top sellers.

➤ Try out our amazing search feature—tell us your favorite theme, setting or time period and we'll find a book that's perfect for you.

All this and more available at

www.eHarlequin.com
on Women.com Networks

SEYRB1

SILHOUETTE'S 20TH ANNIVERSARY CONTEST
OFFICIAL RULES
NO PURCHASE NECESSARY TO ENTER

1. To enter, follow directions published in the offer to which you are responding. Contest begins 1/1/00 and ends on 8/24/00 (the "Promotion Period"). Method of entry may vary. Mailed entries must be postmarked by 8/24/00, and received by 8/31/00.

2. During the Promotion Period, the Contest may be presented via the Internet. Entry via the Internet may be restricted to residents of certain geographic areas that are disclosed on the Web site. To enter via the Internet, if you are a resident of a geographic area in which Internet entry is permissible, follow the directions displayed on-line, including typing your essay of 100 words or fewer telling us "Where In The World Your Love Will Come Alive." On-line entries must be received by 11:59 p.m. Eastern Standard time on 8/24/00. Limit one e-mail entry per person, household and e-mail address per day, per presentation. If you are a resident of a geographic area in which entry via the Internet is permissible, you may, in lieu of submitting an entry on-line, enter by mail, by hand-printing your name, address, telephone number and contest number/name on an 8"x 11" plain piece of paper and telling us in 100 words or fewer "Where In The World Your Love Will Come Alive," and mailing via first-class mail to: Silhouette 20th Anniversary Contest, (in the U.S.) P.O. Box 9069, Buffalo, NY 14269-9069; (In Canada) P.O. Box 637, Fort Erie, Ontario, Canada L2A 5X3. Limit one 8"x 11" mailed entry per person, household and e-mail address per day. On-line and/or 8"x 11" mailed entries received from persons residing in geographic areas in which Internet entry is not permissible will be disqualified. No liability is assumed for lost, late, incomplete, inaccurate, nondelivered or misdirected mail, or misdirected e-mail, for technical, hardware or software failures of any kind, lost or unavailable network connection, or failed, incomplete, garbled or delayed computer transmission or any human error which may occur in the receipt or processing of the entries in the contest.

3. Essays will be judged by a panel of members of the Silhouette editorial and marketing staff based on the following criteria:

   > Sincerity (believability, credibility)—50%
   > Originality (freshness, creativity)—30%
   > Aptness (appropriateness to contest ideas)—20%

   Purchase or acceptance of a product offer does not improve your chances of winning. In the event of a tie, duplicate prizes will be awarded.

4. All entries become the property of Harlequin Enterprises Ltd., and will not be returned. Winner will be determined no later than 10/31/00 and will be notified by mail. Grand Prize winner will be required to sign and return Affidavit of Eligibility within 15 days of receipt of notification. Noncompliance within the time period may result in disqualification and an alternative winner may be selected. All municipal, provincial, federal, state and local laws and regulations apply. Contest open only to residents of the U.S. and Canada who are 18 years of age or older, and is void wherever prohibited by law. Internet entry is restricted solely to residents of those geographical areas in which Internet entry is permissible. Employees of Torstar Corp., their affiliates, agents and members of their immediate families are not eligible. Taxes on the prizes are the sole responsibility of winners. Entry and acceptance of any prize offered constitutes permission to use winner's name, photograph or other likeness for the purposes of advertising, trade and promotion on behalf of Torstar Corp. without further compensation to the winner, unless prohibited by law. Torstar Corp and D.L. Blair, Inc., their parents, affiliates and subsidiaries, are not responsible for errors in printing or electronic presentation of contest or entries. In the event of printing or other errors which may result in unintended prize values or duplication of prizes, all affected contest materials or entries shall be null and void. If for any reason the Internet portion of the contest is not capable of running as planned, including infection by computer virus, bugs, tampering, unauthorized intervention, fraud, technical failures, or any other causes beyond the control of Torstar Corp. which corrupt or affect the administration, secrecy, fairness, integrity or proper conduct of the contest, Torstar Corp. reserves the right, at its sole discretion, to disqualify any individual who tampers with the entry process and to cancel, terminate, modify or suspend the contest or the Internet portion thereof. In the event of a dispute regarding an on-line entry, the entry will be deemed submitted by the authorized holder of the e-mail account submitted at the time of entry. Authorized account holder is defined as the natural person who is assigned to an e-mail address by an Internet access provider, on-line service provider or other organization that is responsible for arranging e-mail address for the domain associated with the submitted e-mail address.

5. Prizes: Grand Prize—a $10,000 vacation to anywhere in the world. Travelers (at least one must be 18 years of age or older) or parent or guardian if one traveler is a minor, must sign and return a Release of Liability prior to departure. Travel must be completed by December 31, 2001, and is subject to space and accommodations availability. Two hundred (200) Second Prizes—a two-book limited edition autographed collector set from one of the Silhouette Anniversary authors: Nora Roberts, Diana Palmer, Linda Howard or Annette Broadrick (value $10.00 each set). All prizes are valued in U.S. dollars.

6. For a list of winners (available after 10/31/00), send a self-addressed, stamped envelope to: Harlequin Silhouette 20th Anniversary Winners, P.O. Box 4200, Blair, NE 68009-4200.

Contest sponsored by Torstar Corp., P.O. Box 9042, Buffalo, NY 14269-9042.